PRINCE HAFIZ'S
ONLY VICE

PRINCE HAFIZ'S ONLY VICE

BY

SUSANNA CARR

First published in Great Britain 2014
by Mills & Boon, an imprint of Harlequin (UK) Limited,
Large Print edition 2015
Eton House, 18-24 Paradise Road,
Richmond, Surrey, TW9 1SR

© 2014 Susanna Carr

ISBN: 978-0-263-25598-0

Printed and bound in Great Britain
by CPI Antony Rowe, Chippenham, Wiltshire

To Sarah Stubbs, with thanks
for her guidance and encouragement.

CHAPTER ONE

HER LOVER'S PICTURE was on the front page of every paper in the small newsstand.

Lacey adjusted the dark sunglasses that concealed her bright blue eyes and squinted at the newspaper on display. Although the headline was in Arabic, the print was big and bold. She could tell that something important had happened. Something that could explain the jubilant attitude that shimmered in the marketplace. No doubt Prince Hafiz had made his countrymen proud again.

She wondered what he had done this time as she requested the daily English paper in halting Arabic. Did he add a fortune to the royal coffers? Convince another industry to make the Sultanate of Rudaynah their headquarters? Win an award?

She decided it would be best to wait until she got home before she read the paper. Lacey took another glance at the pictures of Hafiz that covered the stall. His expression was solemn, but it didn't stop the secret thrill sweeping across her heated skin. It was unnerving that Hafiz could elicit that kind of response through a photograph.

The photo was an official head shot the palace systematically offered to the press, but while the image was familiar, it always grabbed the reader's notice. No one could look away from Prince Hafiz's mysterious dark eyes and harsh mouth. He was devastatingly handsome from his luxuriant black hair to his sharp bone structure. Women watched him from afar, too awed of his masculine beauty.

Or perhaps they sensed his raw power beneath his sophisticated manners. Lacey had instantly recognized the sexual hunger lurking below his ruthless restraint. His primitive aura was a silent warning that most women heeded. But for Lacey, it drew her closer.

She had found Hafiz's relentless self-discipline fascinating. It had also been a challenge. From the moment they had met, she had been tempted to strip him from his exquisitely tailored pin-stripe suit and discover his most sensual secrets.

Just the thought of him made her impatient to get back home. She needed to return before Hafiz got there. His workload would crush a lesser man, but he still managed to visit Lacey at nightfall.

The blazing sun began to dip in the desert sky, and she didn't want to contemplate how Hafiz would respond if she weren't home.

He never asked what she did during the day, Lacey thought with a frown. At first his lack of interest had bothered her. Did he think time stood still for her until he appeared?

There were moments when she wanted to share her plans and ideas, even discuss her day, but she had always held back. She wasn't ready to reveal the work she had done. Not yet. Lacey wanted to show Hafiz what she was capable of. How she could contribute. She wanted to show that she was ready to make his sultanate her permanent home.

It hadn't been easy. There were days, weeks, when she had been homesick. Lonely and bored. She had missed her wide circle of friends and colorful nightlife, and she craved the basic comforts.

It was aggravating that the newspaper hadn't been delivered today at her penthouse, but that wasn't surprising. After living in the small Arabian country for almost six months, Lacey still hadn't gotten used to sporadic service, frequent power outages and laborers arriving at work anywhere from three hours to three days late.

Her connection to the outside world was just as erratic. The communication services were usually down, like today. When they were running, the content was heavily censored.

Definitely not the lifestyle she had enjoyed in St. Louis. Not that she was complaining, Lacey hurriedly assured herself. She was willing to forego many comforts and conveniences for the one thing she couldn't get back in the States: Hafiz.

Lacey shivered with anticipation and handed the coins to the newspaper boy. She practiced her Arabic and felt a sense of accomplishment when the young man understood her. Lacey shyly tugged at the bright orange scarf wrapped around her head and tucked in a wayward strand of hair.

Maybe she was ready to show Hafiz what she had learned over the past few months. She wasn't fluent and didn't know everything about the culture, but she was getting impatient. It was time to meet his family and friends.

Lacey bit her lip as she imagined making that demand. The idea made her uncomfortable. She had been stalling. Not because his family was royal but because she was worried she would push too soon.

Lacey didn't want to give an ultimatum. The last time she'd taken a stand she had lost everything. She wasn't ready to lose Hafiz. Unlike her parents, who had no problems walking away from her in pursuit of their dreams, Hafiz hadn't been able to bear leaving her and had brought her to his home. Well, not his home, but his home country.

As much as she wanted to be part of Hafiz's life and share her life with him, she needed to be patient. She had to trust that Hafiz knew what he was doing. Lacey sighed deeply. She wasn't used to allowing another to take charge.

But she was in a country that followed different codes of conduct. She was also in love with a prince, and she didn't know much about royal life. Her presence in Hafiz's world required delicacy.

Lacey was amazed that Hafiz could even breathe among all the rules and regulations. But not once did he complain. His strong shoulders never sagged from the burden. The man was driven to attack every challenge and reach a goal he never discussed, but Lacey guessed that world domination was just the beginning. His obligations were never far from his mind. That is, until he was in bed with her. Then the world stopped as they fulfilled every fantasy their bodies craved and every wish their hearts desired.

Pleasure nestled low in her stomach, beneath the stifling black gabardine caftan. Lacey stuffed the English newspaper into her plastic shopping bag that contained the crimson desert flowers. She hoped the article offered good news, although she couldn't imagine the press saying anything less than flattering.

She hurried off the curb, and the blowing horn of a filthy truck had her jumping back to the sidewalk. Reddish clouds billowed from the dirt road and settled into a fine layer on her soft black boots.

She waved her hand in front of her face, blinking away the grit. Lacey wrinkled her nose at the tart smell of animals, car fumes and rotting sewage. She knew the small country just recently came into wealth, but if this was a decade of progress, she was grateful she hadn't seen the unenlightened country.

A memory flickered of Hafiz talking about

his country when they had first met. He'd spoken with love and pride about the rich heritage and romance of the desert. Hafiz had described the tribal music and the exotic spices lingering in the starry nights. When he'd told the story of how the sultanate had been named after the first sultana, Lacey had thought Rudaynah had to be a romantic paradise.

Never trust a man's idea of romance, Lacey decided as she determinedly stepped into traffic. The high-pitched ring of bicycle bells shrieked in her ears as she zigzagged her way across the street. She dodged a bored donkey pulling a cart of pungent waste matter. A bus whipped past, her plastic bag swatting against one of the male passengers hanging outside the overcrowded and rusted vehicle.

Lacey hurried to her apartment in earnest. Shadows grew longer and darker as the sun dipped precariously closer to the horizon. She nodded a greeting to the armed guards at the gates of the condominium complex. The men, all in olive green uniforms and sporting bushy mustaches, waved her in without a pause in their conversation.

She scurried across the bare courtyard, pausing only as a big insect with a vicious-sounding buzz flew in front of her. Gritting her teeth as she shuddered with revulsion, Lacey turned the corner to access the private elevator that would lead her straight to the penthouse apartment.

She halted when she saw a man waiting for the elevator. Lacey barely had time to gasp as her mind snatched a flurry of disjointed images. A white flowing robe. A golden chord over the white *kaffiyeh* that covered his hair. She didn't need to see the man's face to sense the impenetrable wall of arrogant masculinity. Of power and privilege. There was only one man who enjoyed a life with no limitations or impossibilities.

"Hafiz?" she whispered.

Prince Hafiz ibn Yusuf Qadi whirled around. "Lacey?" He moved forward and stared at her. He slowly blinked and frowned. His sexy and glamorous mistress was wearing a shapeless caftan and a hideous scarf. There wasn't a hint of makeup on her pale face, but she was still a stunning beauty.

"What are you doing down here?" Prince Hafiz plucked off her sunglasses. He needed to see her eyes. He could always tell what she was thinking and feeling when he met her bright blue gaze.

After he snatched the glasses, Hafiz pushed down the head scarf and was rewarded with a cascade of copper-red curls. His fingers flexed. He wanted to touch her hair. Fan it out and allow the last rays of the sun to catch the fiery color. Sink his fingers into the soft weight as he kissed her hard.

Instead, he slowly, reluctantly, let his hand fall to his side. He gripped her sunglasses until the tips of his fingers whitened. He could not touch her. Not here, not in public. One graze, one brush of skin, and he wouldn't stop.

It didn't help that Lacey wanted to greet him with a kiss. The sight of her closed eyes and parted lips whirled him back to the first time he'd seen her. That fateful night he had entered the luxury hotel near the St. Louis waterfront.

The lobby had bustled with activity and there was a piano bar to the side. The deceptively languorous music had caught his attention, but it was her singing that had made him turn around. Soft and clear like the voice of a well-bred lady, but so rich and velvety that it sparked his wicked imagination.

And when he had seen her, his heart had slammed against his ribs. Lacey was an intriguing mix of contrasts. She had looked like an innocent girl, but her voice held a wealth of experience. Her red hair had flowed past her shoulders like a veil, touching the simple blue evening gown. It should have been a modest dress that covered her from her slender neck to her delicate ankles, yet it had lovingly clung to every curve.

Hafiz had known she was trouble, but that hadn't stopped him from walking toward the piano as she'd coaxed a longing note from the ivory keys.

She hadn't seen his approach as she closed her eyes and raised her flushed face to the sky, swept away from the music. And he had allowed her to take him with her.

Hafiz forced himself to the present and away from the untroubled past. His gaze drifted to the voluminous black gown veiling her body from his eyes. For some reason, that irked him. "What are you wearing?"

She opened her eyes and frowned before she placed her hands on her hips. The movement gave him some indication of where the soft swells and curves were underneath her outfit. "I could ask the same about you," she said as her wide eyes roamed over his appearance. "I have never seen you like this. It's straight out of *Lawrence of Arabia.*"

Lacey's voice was deep and husky as the desire shone in her eyes. When she looked at him like that… His skin flushed and pulled tight.

How did this woman make him this hot, this fast, without even touching him?

His body hardened, and he gulped in the hot desert air. He could take Lacey against this hidden corner and capture her cries of ecstasy with his mouth within minutes. All he needed was… Hafiz shook his head slightly. What was he thinking? The last thing he needed was for the sultan to discover he had a mistress living in the shadow of the palace.

"This is a *dishdasha,*" he explained gruffly as he tried to contain the lust that heated his blood. "I wear it for royal functions. Now explain what you are doing outside alone."

She held up her plastic bag and lightly jostled the contents. "I went shopping."

"Shopping," he repeated dully.

"Yes, I wear this whenever I leave the apartment." She glided her hand down the black gabardine with the flair of a game show model demonstrating a prize. "I know Rudaynah only asks tourists to dress modestly, but I don't know if I fall in that category. I'm not quite a tourist, but I'm not quite a resident, am I? I didn't want to take any chances."

Hafiz barely heard the question. *Whenever she left?* She had done this more than once? Routinely? What did she do? Where did she go? And with whom?

It wouldn't be with a man. He knew he could trust Lacey. She had fallen in love with him that first night and saw no reason to deny it.

But he didn't like the possibility that she had a life apart from him. He was the center of her world, and he didn't want that to end. "Whenever you leave?" he asked as his eyebrows dipped into a ferocious frown. "How often do you go out?"

"You don't need to worry about me." Lacey's smile dropped. "Or are you worried that one of your friends or relatives will meet me?"

Hafiz heard the edge in her tone and felt her impatience. He surrendered to the need to touch her and delve his hands into her hair. He needed to feel the connection that sizzled between them.

Hafiz spanned his fingers along the base of her head and tilted her face up. "I thought you spend your days playing your music," he murmured distractedly.

"And dreaming about you?"

"Of course," he said with a slanted smile.

Her smooth brow wrinkled as she considered what he said. "I can think of you while I'm shopping. I'm talented that way."

"No." His sharp tone stanched any argument. "No more excursions. You don't know the language or the country."

"How else am I going to learn if I don't get out and—"

"You have servants who can shop for you. Yes, yes." He held his hand up as she tried to interrupt. "You've already told me. You're not comfortable with the idea of someone waiting on you. But they are here to take care of you."

"You can't hide me inside all the time," she insisted as she pressed her hand against his chest. His heart thudded from her touch. "I'm not Rapunzel."

"I know," he said resignedly. She often mentioned that European fairy tale. She once told him the basic story line, but someday he needed to read it in case there was more he should know.

Lacey leaned against the wall and sighed. Hafiz flattened his hands next to her head, her sunglasses dangling from his loose grasp. He stared at her mouth, his lips stinging with the need to kiss her.

But this was as close as he would allow himself. If he leaned into her softness, he wouldn't leave.

The tip of her tongue swept along her bottom lip. "Hafiz, we're outside," she reminded him, her voice hitching with scandalized excitement. "You shouldn't be this close."

He knew it, but it didn't stop him. She was his one and only vice, and he was willingly addicted. He had already risked everything to be with her. Each day he made the choice to risk everything for her. But now the choice was taken away from him, and it was all coming to an end.

He bent his head and stopped abruptly. He should pull away. Hafiz remained still as he stared at Lacey's mouth. Their ragged breathing sounded loud to his ears. One kiss could bring him peace or could set him on fire. One kiss would lead to another.

As if he were in a trance, Hafiz grazed his fingertips against her brow. He caressed her cheek, wishing it were his mouth on her. Hafiz swallowed hard as he remembered how her skin tasted.

He shouldn't be with her. No, it was more than that. He shouldn't *want* to be with her. Lacey Maxwell was forbidden.

Wanting Lacey went against everything he had been taught. He should only find honorable and chaste women from his sultanate attractive. Yet the only woman he noticed was Lacey.

She was bold and beautiful. Instead of hiding her curves, she flaunted her body. She showed no shame in her desire for him. And instead of trying to tame him, Lacey encouraged the wild streak inside him that he had tried so hard to suffocate.

The sound of his heartbeat pounded in his ears as he stroked Lacey's jaw. She tilted her head, exposing her slender throat. He wanted to sweep his fingers along the elegant column and dip his hand beneath the caftan. He wanted to hear her shallow breaths turn into groans and whispers.

But that would be reckless. Hafiz dragged his thumb against her lips. He traced the shape of her mouth over and over until her lips clung to his skin.

Lacey turned her face away. Hafiz gripped her chin and held her still. With a growl of surrender, he bent down to claim her mouth with his.

"Hafiz," she whispered fiercely. "We will be seen."

That warning could form ice in his sizzling veins like no other. His chest rose and fell as he reined in runaway needs. With great reluctance, he drew away.

"We should leave before one of the neighbors spots me," Lacey said shakily as she pulled the scarf over her head.

Disappointment scored his chest as she tucked her glorious hair away. "I don't like seeing you covered up like this." He never thought about how he would feel seeing his woman veiled, but it felt intrinsically wrong to conceal Lacey's captivating beauty and character.

"Believe me, I don't like wearing it." She reached for her sunglasses. "It's like an oven, but it makes me invisible and that's all that matters."

He flashed a disbelieving look. "Lacey, you could never be invisible."

Her smile was dazzling as she blushed with pleasure. It was as if he had given her the ultimate compliment.

"Take off your scarf," he insisted in a rough whisper. "No one will see. Everyone will be at prayer." Hafiz wondered why he resented the scarf and sunglasses so much that he was willing to risk the chance of discovery. He reached for her arm and pulled her close.

"Don't be too sure. Most people acted like they were ready to celebrate tonight. I don't know why—" The plastic bag fell from her wrist. She bent down to retrieve the contents, and he followed her descent. Her sharp cry startled him.

"Lacey?" He looked down at the cracked cement floor and didn't understand what was wrong when he saw the dark red flowers resting unblemished on the floor. He almost missed the English newspaper with his picture on the front page. The bold headline grabbed him by the throat and hurtled him into despair.

Prince Hafiz to Marry

CHAPTER TWO

LACEY STARED AT the engagement announcement. Her mind refused to comprehend the words. "Marry?" she whispered. Her wild gaze flew to Hafiz's harsh face. "You're getting married?"

She waited in agony as he rose to his full height. He looked very tall and intimidating. Almost like a stranger.

Lacey didn't realize she was holding her breath until he answered. "Yes."

The single word sent her universe into a spiral. "I don't…I don't…" She stared at the headline again, but the pain was too raw, too intense. She hurriedly stuffed the newspaper and flowers back into the bag.

Her hands shook as the rage and something close to fear swirled inside her. Fear of losing everything. Pure anger at the thought of Hafiz with another woman. The fury threatened to overpower her. She wanted to scream at the injustice and claw at something. Stake her claim. Hafiz belonged to her.

"You have been with another woman." She couldn't believe it. "All this time, you were with someone else."

Hafiz's eyes narrowed at the accusation. "No. You have been the only woman in my life since I met you in St. Louis a year ago."

She was the only woman, and yet he was going to marry another? Lacey fumbled with her sunglasses and tossed them in the bag. "Then how are you...I don't understand."

He braced his feet a shoulders' width apart and clasped his hands behind his back, preparing for battle. "I met the bride today and she agreed."

Lacey's mouth gaped open. "You just met her?" She snatched the flicker of hope and held on tight. "So, it's an arranged marriage."

Hafiz let out a bark of humorless laughter. "Of course."

"Then, what's the problem?" She moved slowly as she stood. Her arms and legs felt limp and shaky. She lurched as she stepped on the hem of her insufferable caftan. "Say that you won't get married."

He looked away. "I can't." Regret tinged his voice.

Lacey wanted to stamp her foot and demand a better answer, but she knew she wouldn't get it. Not with his shuttered expression and the regal tilt of his stubborn chin. "It's not like you're the crown prince," she argued, "although I don't understand that since you're the oldest son. But this means you have more freedom."

Hafiz's eyes closed wearily for a brief moment. "For the last time, the sultan chooses the next in line for the throne. My father chose my brother. And, no, I don't have any freedom in this matter, even though I will never rule. In my case, I have less."

She didn't want to hear that. Thick emotions

already clogged her aching throat. "You should never have agreed to marry this woman," she said as her voice wobbled.

He turned his attention back to her. "I gave my consent," he said gently. "I can't take it back."

What about the promises he made to her? The ones he made first. The ones about how they would be together. Didn't those promises matter? Didn't *she* matter?

"Why did you agree in the first place?" She held the plastic bag to her chest. She would rather hold on to something solid and strong like Hafiz until the emotional storm passed, which would still leave her feeling battered and stinging with pain, but he would prevent her from breaking. "You should have refused."

"I couldn't this time." Hafiz winced the moment he revealed too much. He pressed his lips into a straight line.

Lacey stared at him with open suspicion. "This time?" she echoed. "How long have you been looking for a wife?"

"Could we not discuss this here?" he bit out

tersely. "Let's go back to the apartment." He guided her to the elevator, keeping a firm hand on her arm as she still weaved from the unpleasant shock. He pressed the call button, and she watched as if her life depended on it, but her brain couldn't register the simple, everyday action.

"Marry," she repeated and shook her head. "I don't believe this. Why didn't you tell me?"

"I am telling you." He kept his eyes on the descending lighted floor numbers.

"Now. After everything is settled." She couldn't be bothered to hide the accusation in her voice.

He spared a glance at her. "Not quite, but it is official as of this morning. I wanted to tell you before you found out from another source."

That explained the missing newspapers. "How considerate." She felt his start of surprise from her bitter sarcasm, but she didn't care. Hafiz was getting married. To someone else. The knowledge stabbed at her heart. It was a wonder she didn't break from the piercing force. "When is the wedding taking place?"

"After Eid." His answer was almost swallowed by the clank and thump of the arriving elevator.

Eid. That holiday came after the month of Ramadan, if she recalled correctly. She remembered something being mentioned in the paper about that coming soon. "Three months?" she made a guess.

He held the sliding metal doors open for her. "More or less."

Lacey walked into the elevator compartment, her head spinning. Three months. She only had three months with Hafiz.

What was she thinking? She had no more time left. Oh, God. She wasn't strong enough to handle this. She was going to shatter from the pain. Hafiz was an engaged man. Off-limits. And she never had any warning.

Her mouth suddenly felt dry as she instinctively pressed the burgeoning wails and sobs into silence until they were ready to burst from her skin. "You should have told me you were looking for a wife."

"I wasn't. I have no interest in getting married. I held it off for as long as possible."

Lacey reeled back in shock. Hafiz had no interest in marriage? *At all?* Not even to her? If that was the case, then what had the past six months been about?

"My parents were looking for a wife for me," he clarified sternly.

"But you knew they were," she argued. "You knew this was going to happen."

Hafiz said nothing and pressed the top floor button several times as the elevator doors slowly shut.

Winning that point of the argument was a hollow victory. "How long have they been looking?" A part of her wanted to know, the other part wanted to deny that any of this was happening.

He stood silently, his jaw tightly clenched. A muscle twitched in his cheek. Lacey thought for a moment he didn't hear her and was about to repeat the question when he finally answered. "A couple of years."

"A…couple of *years*?" She couldn't possibly have heard that correctly. Lacey folded her arms across her chest. "From the time that you knew me, from the very first time you *propositioned* me, you were also on the marriage market? And not once did you find the chance to tell me?"

Why would he? Lacey thought bitterly. He hadn't considered her to be in the running. She was just a bit of fun on the side. A temporary distraction. Oh, she was a fool.

"Marriage negotiations are delicate and complex," he explained as impatience roughened his words. "It could have taken even longer to find a suitable match."

Suitable. She sneered at the term. It was a code word for the right bloodline and the right upbringing from the right family. Not a blue-eyed American who was also an unemployed nightclub musician.

Oh, and suitable meant someone who was pure and virginal. She mustn't forget that.

The injustice of it all flared to new heights. "Not once did you tell me, and yet I dropped my entire life to be with you." Her voice raised another octave. "I moved to the far-off corners of the earth, to this hell—"

"The Sultanate of Rudaynah is not hell." His low growl was similar to that of a wild cat ready to pounce.

"—And exist solely for you and your pleasure! And you don't have the decency to tell me that you're getting married?" Her eyes narrowed into a withering glare.

He gestured with his hands. "Calm down."

"Calm down?" She thought now was as good a time as any to rant. She was ready to punctuate her tantrum by throwing her shopping bag at his sinfully gorgeous face. "Calm down! No, I will not calm down. The man I love, the man I sacrificed everything for is throwing it all away right back into my face," she hissed, her cheeks hot with fury. "Believe me, this is not a time to calm down."

Hafiz was suddenly in front of her. He made

a grab for her, but she raised her hands, warding him off. Lacey fought the urge to burrow her head into his shoulder and weep.

"I am not throwing you away, damn it. How could I?" he asked as his bronze eyes silently pleaded for understanding. "You are the best thing that has ever happened to me."

Lacey looked away and tilted her head against the corner. She needed something to lean against anyway as her knees were incapable of supporting her. A buzzing filled her head. She took short, even breaths of the stifling air and blinked back the dark spots.

As the elevator made its slow, rocky ascent, Lacey realized that Hafiz must be equally unnerved by the turn of the events. He had cursed. Another first for the day. Hafiz never, ever cursed. But then, he always controlled the situation and his environment with the same iron will he used over his temper.

Over himself, really. The man never drank alcohol or gambled. He did not live in excess. His sculpted muscles were that of an athlete in training. He barely slept, too busy working to improve the living conditions of Rudaynah. When he wasn't fulfilling his royal and patriotic duties, he met every family obligation. Even marry his parent's choice.

The only time he went wild, the only time he allowed his control to slip, was when they were in bed. Lacey winced, and the first scalding teardrop fell.

Tears streamed out of her eyes and burned jagged lines down her hot cheeks. Why had she thought Hafiz was considering a future with her? Not once did he mention the possibility of happily-ever-after. Never did the word "marriage" ever cross his lips.

But the dream had been harbored deep in her heart, secretly growing. It had been incredibly naïve and wrong to think all she had to do was be patient. She thought that if she came here and slowly entered the culture, she would eventually stand publicly by Hafiz's side as his wife.

Only that dream died the moment Hafiz pledged himself to another. She gasped as the words plunged into her heart. The surrounding blackness she had been fighting back swiftly invaded her mind.

Pledged to another...

The buzzing grew louder and almost masked Hafiz's shout of alarm.

"Lacey!" Hafiz caught her as she slid down the wall. He plucked off her scarf, and her head lolled to one side. He supported her head with his shoulder and noted that her unnaturally pale face was sticky with sweat. He patted her clammy cheek with his hand. "Lacey," he repeated, trying to rouse her.

Her eyelashes fluttered. "So hot."

He gathered her in his arms. The ill-fitting black gown bunched around her slender figure. "I'll take care of you," he promised, holding her tighter. And he would, he vowed to himself, until his last breath. No matter what she thought, he would never cast her aside.

The elevator finally stopped on the penthouse floor. He searched her features, vaguely aware how her curly long hair hung defiantly like a copper flag and her bare legs dangled from the crook of his elbow, exposing her ivory skin for the world to see. If they were caught in this compromising embrace, so be it. Lacey's safety and comfort were always top priority, but now it was more essential than his next heartbeat, Hafiz decided as he stepped out of the elevator and onto the open-air hallway to the apartment.

The sun was setting. Dark reds and rich purples washed the sky as evening prayers were sung from a nearby loudspeaker. Hafiz kept his eyes out for any potential trouble, but he saw no one strolling the grounds or outside the condominiums across the courtyard. But from the domestic sounds emitting from the neighbors' homes on the other floors, the situation could change in an instant.

Carrying Lacey to her front door at a brisk pace, Hafiz noted he wasn't even breathing hard from lifting her. She weighed barely anything. He glanced down at her face and the fragility struck him like a fist.

Not for the first time did he wonder if moving Lacey to Rudaynah had been the best decision for her. Life in hiding had taken its toll. Why hadn't he seen that before? Or did he not want to see it?

Lacey stirred as if she was acutely aware of his perusal. "I'm fine," she murmured and tentatively ran her tongue over her parched lips.

"No, you're not." He leaned heavily against the doorbell and waited at the iron grille door until the American servant wearing a loose T-shirt and cargo pants came to the door.

"Your Highness! What happened?" Glenn asked as he unlocked the door bolts with economical movements. His craggy face showed no alarm, but his watchful eyes were alert. His body, lean from many years of military training, vibrated with readiness to act on the first command from his employer.

"It's all right. She fainted from the heat." Hafiz kicked off his sandals at the door and moved past the older man. "I'll get her into the shower. Have your wife prepare something very cold and sweet for her to drink."

"I'm sorry, Your Highness." Glenn raked his hand over his bristly gray hair. "She said—"

"It's all right," he repeated, calling over his shoulder as he made way to the master bedroom. "Lacey has always had a problem following directions."

"I'm not dead, you know," Lacey said with her eyes closed. "I can hear every word."

"Good, because I do not want you venturing outside again without Glenn," Hafiz said as he stepped into the large room where he spent many hours exploring Lacey's body and revealing the darkest recesses of his heart. This time the sumptuous silks and oversized pillows didn't stir his hot blood. He wanted to tuck Lacey between the colorful sheets and not let her out of bed until she regained her vibrancy. "He is your bodyguard and—"

"He is to play the role of my next of kin if any questions are asked because single women are not allowed to travel alone in this country,"

Lacey ended in a monotone. She let out a slow, stuttering sigh that seemed to originate from somewhere deep inside her. "I know."

"Then, don't let it happen again." He pushed the bathroom door open with his bare foot. Slapping the light switch outside the door with the palm of his hand, he entered the window-less room now flooding with light.

"It won't."

The determination in her voice made him hesitate. He cautiously watched her face as he set her down gently, sliding her feminine curves along his length. For once her expression showed nothing. Her eyes veiled her feelings. Usually her eyes would darken with righteous indignation, glow with rapturous delight and twinkle with every emotion in between. The sudden change in her behavior troubled him.

He wanted to hold her close until he could read her thoughts, but Lacey had other ideas as she moved away from him. "Can you stand on your own?" he asked.

"Yes." She took another step back and shucked

off her cloth boots. The movements lacked her usual energy.

He kept one hand outstretched in case he had to catch her as he started the shower full blast. Hafiz turned his attention on Lacey and quickly divested her of her black caftan.

"Lacey!" His startled hoarse cry echoed in the small room. The sight of her barely-there peach lingerie was a shocking contrast against the conservative cloth. Hafiz's body reacted immediately. The heavy black material dropped from his fists and flopped on the wet floor.

"What?" She inspected her arms and legs. "What's wrong?"

He cleared his throat, wishing he could also clear the sharp arousal tightening his body. "You're supposed to wear several layers of clothes under the caftan." He unhooked the front closure of her bra, his knuckles grazing her breast. He saw the tremor in his hands. He was acting like a callow youth.

"Are you kidding?" She skimmed the high-cut

panties down her legs and kicked them aside. "I would boil alive."

His gaze traveled as the peach satin landed on the black fabric. The searing image branded in his mind. The way he would look at women in the shapeless caftan was forever changed. He swallowed roughly as he controlled his baser instinct. "What if you had gotten caught?"

"No one would have found out. You are the only person who has shown enough nerve to get that close." She arched her eyebrow in disapproval.

And he was going to keep it that way. "Here, get under the water." He pulled her to the showerhead.

"Oh! Ow!" Lacey squealed in dismay as the icy cold spray hit her body. She jumped back and rubbed her hands over her arms. "This is so cold."

"You'll get used to it in just a minute," he replied as he always did to her comments on the lack of heated water. The familiarity calmed him while her beaded nipples made his brain sluggish.

"You can leave now," she said through chattering teeth. She looked away from him and tested the temperature by dipping her foot in the cold water.

He leaned against the door and folded his arms across his chest. "I don't want you passing out in the shower."

"I won't. Now go before your royal gown gets soaked." She shooed him away with her hands.

She had a point. The bathroom, already hot as a sauna, was in the traditional Rudaynahi design, with the exception of a European commode. The concrete floor had a drain and was also to be used as the shower floor. Since there was no plastic curtain or glass shower door, the water was already spraying every inch of the bathroom.

"If you're sure," Hafiz said and flashed a wicked smile. "But I can just as easily take it off."

She glared back at him. "I'm sure."

His smile turned wry at her ungracious rejection. He shouldn't have made the offer. He knew that but went for it anyway. "I'll be outside," Hafiz said. Lacey didn't respond as she stuck her head fully under the spray.

He stepped out of the bathroom and almost collided with the housekeeper who carried a small tray into the bedroom. The tall frosty glass of juice rattled against a plate of figs and dates.

"How is she doing?" Annette asked as she set the tray on the bedside table. "Do we need to call a doctor?"

"No, she's not sick." The uncertain look of the older woman irritated him. If he truly felt Lacey needed medical care, he would call the American doctor who'd already discovered that cashing in favors from a prince was worth more than any currency in a country that relied heavily on the bartering system.

The physician was brilliant and up to date on medicine. Hafiz had seen that firsthand when Lacey arrived in the country and had drunk water that had not been purified. That week had been torture, and Hafiz was insistent that she was given the best care, no matter what. Hafiz would never place secrecy above Lacey's well-being, and it stung to have someone silently questioning his priorities.

"She's overheated," he explained, keeping the defensiveness out of his voice. "The shower is already doing wonders."

"We threw away the newspapers like you requested, but we never thought Lacey would leave to get one." The woman twisted the pleat of her yellow sundress with nervous hands and slid a worried glance at the closed bathroom door.

"It's no one's fault," he said. No one's but his own. He should have prepared Lacey for the possibility of his wedding, but he'd held on to the hope that his intended bride would have declined the offer. "Please, find something light for her to wear."

"Of course." The housekeeper gratefully accepted the task and opened the doors to the armoire, revealing gossamer-thin cotton in every color of the rainbow.

Hafiz walked into the simply appointed drawing room and tried to recapture the peace he always felt whenever he stepped into this home. Decorated with an eclectic mix of wood tables carved in the severe Rudaynahi style and chunky upholstered sofas from the Western world, Lacey had managed to add her upbeat personality with tribal throw rugs and colorful paintings from local artisans.

The apartment was more than a home. It was a haven. It was the only place he felt both passion and peace. The only place in the world he experienced unconditional love.

Hafiz walked slowly to the grand piano that sat in the middle of the room and under the carefully positioned spotlight. It had been incredibly difficult shipping the instrument into the country. Flying in a piano tuner every couple of months was no easy feat, but seeing Lacey's joy and listening to her soulful music made it all worthwhile.

He fingered the sheet music scattered on the polished black wood. The woman had the talent to become a successful recording artist. Hafiz had told her enough times, but she always shook her head in disagreement. Music was a big part of her, but she didn't want to be consumed with the ladder of success like her parents, who were still striving for their big break. She didn't have the desire.

But she stored up all her passion for him. Did that make him feel less guilty in whisking her to his country? The edges of the sheet music crinkled under his fingertips. Because she had no interest in pursuing a career? Because she didn't have family ties?

Hafiz pondered the question as he walked to the doors leading to the balcony that overlooked the Persian Gulf. He admitted that it made it easier to ask her to drop everything and follow him. To stay in the apartment and wait for him. Not once had she complained or shown resentment until today.

And she had every right. He had risked everything for more time with Lacey. The relation-ship they had was forbidden. And now, as of today, it was impossible.

Only Hafiz didn't allow that word in his vo-cabulary, and he wasn't willing to let the idea invade his life with Lacey.

"What are you still doing here?" Lacey asked at the doorway on the other side of the long room.

Hafiz turned around. Lacey's wet hair was slicked back into a copper waterfall. She had changed into a pink cotton caftan that clung to her damp skin. Gold threads were woven into the fabric and sparkled like stars.

"Are you feeling better?" he asked, silently watching the housekeeper duck into the kitchen.

"Much. You're free to go." She walked toward the front door.

"Lacey, we need to talk."

"No kidding, but I don't want to right now." She gripped the thick door handle. "You have had years to think about this. I have had less than an hour."

"Lacey—" He crossed the room and stood in front of her, prepared to take the brunt of her anger and soak up her tears.

"I want you to go." She flung open the door.

Hafiz's shoulders flexed with tension. Every instinct told him to stay, but he knew what she said made sense. It was strange to have her as the calm one and he filled with impetuous emotions. He didn't like the role reversal.

Hafiz agreed with a sharp nod. "I will be here tomorrow after work." He leaned down to brush her cheek with a gentle kiss.

She turned her head abruptly. "Don't." Her eyes focused on the hallway outside the iron grille.

His heart stopped. Lacey had never rejected his touch. "What are you saying?" he asked in a low voice as his lungs shriveled, unable to take in the next breath.

The muscles in her throat jerked. "You shouldn't touch me." The words were a mere whisper. "The moment you became engaged, the moment you chose another woman, we no longer exist."

Hafiz grasped her chin between his thumb and forefinger. "You don't mean that," he said, staring at her intensely. As if he could change her mind through his sheer willpower.

"Yes, I do."

He swallowed down the rising fear. "Obviously, you are still suffering from your collapse." The tip of his thumb caressed the angry line of her bottom lip.

Lacey yanked away from his touch. "I'm thinking quite clearly. You made your choice." She took a step back behind the door, shielding herself from him. "And this is mine."

"You are going to regret those words. You can't send me away." He stepped toward her, ready to prove it.

Lacey's glare was so cold it could have frozen the desert air seeping into the apartment. "Do you want me to cause a scene in front of this complex to get you to leave?"

Her threat surprised Hafiz. That wasn't like

her. She knew his weak spots but had always protected him. Now she was so angry, she was becoming a dangerous woman.

Would she try to hurt him because he was getting married? No, not Lacey. She was loyal to him…but when she thought she didn't have any competition. How could he convince her that this marriage was in name only?

He decided to change his strategy. "I will return," he said, shoving his feet into his sandals. The expensive leather threatened to snap under his angry motions. "And you will be here waiting for me."

Defiance flared in her blue eyes. "Don't tell me what to do. You have no right."

"You still belong to me, Lacey," he announced as he left. "Nothing and no one will change that."

CHAPTER THREE

THE WHITE ROBES slapped angrily against Hafiz's legs as he stormed into his office. He would rather be anywhere else but here. Although the palace's murky shadows descending on the spartan rooms were good companions to his dark mood this evening.

"Your Highness." His private secretary clumsily hung up the phone. The withered old man bowed low, his fragile bones creaking. "His Majesty wishes to speak to you."

Hafiz set his jaw as dread seeped inside him. The day couldn't get any worse. The sultan didn't command appointments from his eldest offspring unless there was or would be an unpleasant event.

"When did he make this request?"

"Ten minutes ago, Your Highness," the elderly man answered, his focus on the thread-bare Persian rug. "I called your cell phone and left several messages."

Of course. He had turned off his phone so he wouldn't bend to the overwhelming need to call Lacey. His show of confidence that she would follow his orders was going to cost him in more ways than one. Hafiz wanted to roar with frustration, but he needed to stay calm and focused for the sultan.

Hafiz turned and checked his appearance in the gilt-edged mirror. He didn't see anything Sultan Yusuf would find offensive, but the ruler didn't need to hunt long for something to disapprove about his son. Unable to delay the inevitable, Hafiz set his shoulders back and strode to the palace offices.

When he entered the sultan's suite, Hafiz stood respectfully at the double doors and waited to be announced. As one of the secretaries hurried to the massive wooden desk to convey the message to the sultan, Hafiz grew aware of the sideway glances and growing tension. He coldly met the employees' stares one by one until the gazes skittered down in belated respect.

Sultan Yusuf dismissed his secretaries with the flick of his hand. The men hurried past Hafiz and through the doors. Their expressions of grateful relief concerned him.

The sultan continued to sit behind his desk and read a note on thick white paper. He took his time to deign to acknowledge his son's presence. "Hafiz," Sultan Yusuf finally said.

Hafiz approached the sultan. "Your Majesty." Hafiz gave the briefest deferential nod as defiance flowed through his veins.

The sultan tossed the paper on to his desk. "Be seated."

The lack of mind games made Hafiz suspicious, which it was probably supposed to achieve. Hafiz sat down on the chair across from the desk. Tradition dictated that he should keep his head down and his gaze averted. He was never good at tradition.

The sultan leaned back in his chair, steepled

his fingers, and studied Hafiz. Not even a whisper of affection crossed his lined face. "You are very fortunate that the Abdullah daughter agreed to the marriage."

Fortune had nothing to do with it. It didn't matter who his bride was. He was marrying this woman for two reasons. It was his royal duty and it was another step toward redemption.

"This girl knows about your—" the king's fingers splayed apart "—misspent youth, as does her family."

Hafiz clenched his teeth and willed his hands to stay straight on his knees. He would not respond. He would not allow his father to spike his temper.

"They will use that knowledge to their advantage as the wedding preparations draw closer. The dowry is not nearly worthy enough for a prince. We're fortunate they didn't demand a bridal price."

Hafiz still said nothing. His teeth felt as if they would splinter. His fingers itched to curl and dig into his knees.

"Have you anything to say, Hafiz?"

He did, but most of it wasn't wise to say aloud. "I regret that my past mistakes still cost our family." And his regret was as honest as it was strong. Nothing could erase the suffering he'd caused Rudaynah. The simple truth destroyed him, and his life's mission was to prevent any future suffering from his hand.

"As do I." Sultan Yusuf sighed heavily. "The reason I'm telling you this is that I expect many maneuvers from the Abdullah family." He smacked his lips with distaste as he mentioned his future in-laws. "Any male relative could trick you. Talk you down the dowry. Say you made a promise or agreement when there was none."

Annoyance welled up inside Hafiz's chest. From years of practice, his expression didn't show his feelings. Hafiz negotiated multi-million-dollar deals, brokered delicate international agreements and increased the wealth of this country ten times over. But his family didn't respect his accomplishments. They only remembered his mistakes.

"You will have no interaction with the Abdullah family," the sultan commanded. "All inquiries must be directed to my office. Do you understand, Hafiz?"

"Yes, Your Majesty." He didn't have a problem following that order. If that was the purpose of the meeting, Hafiz wondered why the sultan didn't dictate a memo so he didn't have to speak to his son.

"After all," the ruler continued, "your mother and I cannot afford another scandal from you."

Hafiz closed his eyes as the pain washed over him. He should have seen that coming.

"This marriage must happen." The sultan tapped an authoritative finger on the desk. The thud echoed loudly in Hafiz's head. "If the engagement is broken, it will shame this family."

Shaming the family was his sole specialty. The statement was left unspoken, but Hafiz could hear it plainly in his father's manner. It wasn't anything his conscience hadn't shouted for more years than he cared to remember.

"You've already lost your right to the throne

because of your poor choices," Sultan Yusuf said with brutal frankness. "If you harm this agreement, I will make certain you lose everything you hold dear."

Did his father think he would try to sabotage the wedding agreement? Hafiz was stunned at the possibility. Hadn't his actions proven he would sacrifice his personal wants for the good of the country?

"But, if you do not cause any delay or scandal—" he paused and sliced a knowing look "—I will give you the one thing you desire."

Hafiz flinched. His mind immediately went to Lacey. A white-hot panic blinded him. Did the sultan know about her?

"Marry the bride I choose, and you will resume your rightful place. You will become the heir to the throne once again."

Lacey's fingers dragged against the ivory keys of her piano, but she didn't play a note. She couldn't. The music inside her had been silenced.

Glenn and Annette had retired hours ago, but she couldn't sleep no matter how hard she tried. Her body felt limp and wrung out, and her mind craved for oblivion.

What was it about her? Why was she so easy to discard? First her parents and now Hafiz. She didn't understand it.

Lacey always held on to the belief that she would have bonded with her parents if they had taken her on the road with them. They would have remembered her birthdays and special occasions. They wouldn't have forgotten her all those times or accidentally left her to fend for herself on school vacations. If they hadn't sent her off to live with distant relatives or family friends, she would have some sort of relationship today with her mother and father.

But now she knew her parents didn't get the full blame. There was something wrong with her. It didn't matter how freely and completely she gave her love; she would not get it in return. She was unlovable.

Lacey stood and walked to the balcony doors

and peered outside. No lights glowed against the darkness. Outside appeared silent and empty.

If only her mind would quiet down like the town below her. She leaned her head against the glass pane that was now cool from the desert night. The moment Hafiz had left, fragmented thoughts and fears had bombarded her mind. She'd paced her room as unspoken questions whirled through her head. She'd stared numbly at the walls for hours.

No matter how much the housekeeper had tried to tempt her with food, Lacey refused to eat. Her throat, swollen and achy from crying, would surely choke on the smallest morsel. Sustenance meant nothing and she had curled up on Hafiz's side of the bed. There she had muffled her cries in his pillow when one more minute of living without him became unbearable.

Her mind felt as chaotic as the clothes jumbled inside her suitcase. She packed her belongings, which were pathetically few. It was a mocking symbol of the emptiness of her life before she'd met Hafiz and her barren future without him.

Only now she had even less, because she was leaving everything behind along with her heart.

Lacey frowned, trying to hold her emotions together. There were too many things she had to do, like finding a new home.

Lacey pressed the heels of her hands against her puffy eyes. The business of breaking up was beyond her. She needed a fresh start. Somewhere that held no memories. A place where Hafiz couldn't find her.

Not that he would follow her across the world. He'd made his choice. And it wasn't her. It was never going to be her.

She didn't want to know anything about the woman who got to share Hafiz's life. The one who would wear his ring, bear his name and carry his children in her womb. Lacey blinked as her eyes stung, but she'd already used up her tears.

Lacey twisted around when she heard the key in the lock. Hope stuttered through her exhausted body as Hafiz entered. He halted when he saw her across the room.

"Hafiz." She instinctively moved toward him like a moth to a flame. "What are you doing here?"

She stared at him, memorizing every detail. He was dressed like a laborer. While the outfit was an unusual choice for a member of the royal family, Hafiz lent a sophisticated elegance to the rough work clothes.

The simple tunic was as black as his short hair. The cotton sluiced down his muscular chest and skimmed past his knees. His jeans strained against his powerful legs as he slid his feet out of scuffed sandals. His high-tech watch was nowhere to be found, but the royal ring gleamed proudly on his hand.

"I wasn't sure you would be here." His hands clenched and unclenched the keys.

Lacey guiltily flashed a look in the direction of the bedroom where her bags were packed and stowed away under the bed. "And you're checking up on me?" she asked as her eyebrows arched with disbelief. "You could have called."

"No. I came here to say goodbye." He set

down the key with hypnotic slowness. "To-night."

She froze as the words pummeled her bruised heart. Tonight? Her chest heaved, and she struggled for her next breath. "Now?"

Hafiz nodded. "I had a meeting with the sultan earlier this evening." He stared at the keys as though he wanted to snatch them back. "If any of my actions prevent the forthcoming marriage, I will lose everything."

"Your father threatened you?" she whispered in horror.

"The sultan warned me," he corrected. "And I can't help but wonder if he knows about you. Maybe not your name or where you live, but that I have someone like you in my life."

Someone like you... The phrase scratched at her. What did that mean? More importantly, what did it mean to Hafiz?

She stood in front of him, and placed her hand on his arm, offering him comfort. Not that he needed it. Hafiz had the strength to stand alone.

"You shouldn't be forced to marry someone you don't love."

Her words seemed to startle him. "Lacey," Hafiz said in a groan as he cupped her cheek with his hand. "A royal marriage never has anything to do with love. It has always been that way."

She closed her eyes as she leaned into his hand, knowing it would be the last time he would caress her. She gathered the last of her self-discipline and withdrew from his touch. Energy arced and flared between them.

"I will miss you, Hafiz," she said brokenly as her throat closed up. The tears she thought couldn't happen beaded on her eyelashes.

Hafiz let out a shuddering breath. He swept his fingertip against the corner of her eye, taking her tears with him. The moisture clung to his knuckle, and he rubbed it into his skin with his thumb, silently sharing her agony.

The image took a chink out of her hard-earned resolve. Lacey wrapped her arms around her stomach before she crumbled altogether. "I had so many questions to ask you, and now I can't remember what they were." All except for one that danced on her tongue. "Did you ever love me?"

Silence throbbed in the air.

Lacey blinked at the question that had tumbled from her mouth. *Of all the things to ask,* her mind screamed.

Hafiz went unnaturally still.

"I don't know why I asked." She shrugged as her pain intensified. "Please, don't answer that."

The words were ripped from deep within her. She desperately wanted to know the answer. She never questioned it before, but she had been living in a fantasy.

Lacey had always felt Hafiz loved her. It was in his touch, in his eyes, and in his smile. But he never said the words, even when she chanted her declaration of love in the height of ecstasy.

It was too late to find out. If he didn't love her, she would never recover. If he did love her, then she would never let go. Even if he was married, even if he kept her hidden. And she couldn't let that happen.

Hafiz frowned. "Lacey…"

"Ssh." She silenced him by pressing her fingers against his parted lips. *"Please."*

He covered her hand with his and placed soft kisses in the heart of her palm. "I don't want you to leave," he said against her skin.

"Then, come away with me!" She impulsively tangled her fingers with his and pulled him away from the door. His torn expression shamed her. She drew back and let go of his hand. "I'm sorry. That was wrong."

He moved swiftly and crushed her against him. "I can't leave Rudaynah," he whispered, his breath ruffling her hair. "And you can't stay. I don't know what I'm going to do without you. I'm only half alive when you are not around."

He didn't want to give her up, but he had the strength to do it when she wanted to ignore the inevitable. Hafiz would flourish without her while she wilted into a slow death. "In time, you'll forget all about me."

He tightened their embrace. "How can you say that?"

"You will," she predicted with a sigh. It happened to her before, and nothing she did would stop it from happening again. "You need to leave." Now, before it became impossible. Before she threw herself at his feet and begged him to stay.

"Yes." He gradually relaxed his hold but didn't let go. "This was already a risk."

She looked up into his face. The scent of the desert night clung to his warm skin. The steady and strong beat of his heart pounded under her hand. The passion he felt for her shone in his eyes. This was how she wanted to remember him. "Goodbye, Hafiz."

He lowered his face and gently brushed his mouth against hers. Like Lacey, he kept his eyes open, needing to commit this last kiss to memory. The unshed tears in her eyes blurred his image. Lacey's lips clung to his. The craving to deepen the kiss radiated between them. She felt his need to carry her away and the struggle to leave her behind.

"I have to go," he murmured against her mouth.

"I know." The world tilted as he withdrew, and his arms dropped away from her. She felt exposed and weak. A single tear spilled down her cheek. "I wish…" She stopped and bit her lip.

"You wish what?" When she didn't answer, he grabbed her upper arms with his large hands. "Tell me," he pleaded, his fingers biting into her flesh.

"No." She shook her head. She had to be strong and ignore her wants. For both of them. "I wish you…happiness."

Hafiz shook her slightly until tendrils of her hair fell in front of her face. "That was not what you were going to say. Don't end this on a lie," he ordered, agony threading his voice. "Don't leave me with a half-spoken wish, so that I will go mad trying to figure out what you wanted to say."

Lacey looked away. She'd ruined the moment, all because she couldn't let him go. "I can't."

"Tell me what you wish," he said against her ear, teasing her willpower with his husky voice full of promise. "I will make it come true if it's in my power."

"I wish we…" She swallowed. Damn her weakness! "I wish we had at least one more night."

She saw the gleam in Hafiz's bronze eyes. Her request unleashed something dark and primitive inside him. He wanted to claim her, possess her so completely that she would never forget him. As if she could.

"I can grant you that wish," he promised as his features sharpened with lust. "Tonight."

"No." Lacey shook her head. They had to stop now. If she went to bed with him tonight, she would do everything in her power to keep him there. "We can't. You are an engaged man. The sultan has warned you—"

"This is my wish, too." He gathered her close and lifted her in his arms before he strode to the bedroom. "Don't deny me one more night."

CHAPTER FOUR

LACEY CLUNG TO Hafiz as they entered her bedroom. The bedside lamp offered a faint glow in the large room, casting shadows on the unmade bed. Hafiz barely broke his stride when he kicked the door shut.

She wasn't sure why he wasn't rushing to the bed. Lacey felt the urgency pulsating between them. This was the last time they would be together. They had to get a lifetime into one night.

The unfairness of it all hit Lacey, and she tried to push it away. She didn't want to focus on that. She wasn't going to waste her last moments with Hafiz on something she couldn't control.

The only thing she could do was make one beautiful and lasting memory. Have something that could ease the pain when she thought about the love she lost.

Hafiz stood by the edge of the bed, and Lacey knelt on the mattress before him. She pressed her hands against his cheeks and looked deep into his eyes.

She bit the inside of her lip to prevent from speaking when she saw Hafiz's sadness. It wasn't like him to show it, but the emotion was too strong; he couldn't contain it. Lacey closed her eyes and rested her head against his chest. She wanted to ease his pain. Take it away from him.

She was hurting, too. It hurt knowing that after tonight she wouldn't see him, and she couldn't touch him. She wouldn't be allowed anywhere near him.

Her shaky breath echoed in the room.

"Lacey?" Hafiz's voice was tender as he smoothed his hand against the crown of her head.

She tilted her face up and sought his mouth. She poured everything she felt into the kiss. She held nothing back. The pain and the anger. The love and the unfulfilled dreams.

The heat between them wasn't a slow burn. It flared hot and wild. Lacey sensed the dangerous power behind it, but this time she didn't care. In the past they danced around it, knowing it could rage out of control. This time she welcomed it. Encouraged it.

Hafiz bunched her caftan in his fists. She knew it was a silent warning. He needed to leash his sexual hunger, or it could become destructive.

She didn't think that was possible. There was nothing left to destroy. She wanted to climb the heights with Hafiz and disregard the possibility of plunging into the depths.

Lacey wrenched her mouth away from Hafiz. Her breath was uneven as her chest rose and fell. She watched him as she tore off her caftan, revealing that she wore nothing underneath.

As she tossed her clothes on to the floor, a part of her warned her to slow down. This was not what she wanted their last night to be like. She wanted it soft and romantic. This was primal and elemental. And she couldn't stop. She didn't *want* to slow down.

Hafiz shucked off his tunic, exposing his muscular chest. She reached out with the intention to trail her hand down his warm, golden skin. Instead she hooked her hand over the low-slung waistband of his jeans and pulled him close. She gasped as the tips of her breasts rubbed against his coarse chest hair.

Hafiz stretched his arms and wrapped his hands around the bedposts. His move surprised her. He didn't gather her close or take over. He was giving the control to her.

It was a rare gift. Hafiz was always in control. She watched him as she boldly cupped his arousal. A muscle bunched in his jaw, but he said nothing. He didn't move as she teased him with her hands. She lowered the zipper and pushed his clothes down his legs.

She wasn't gentle as she stroked him. She felt the tension rise inside him and felt the bedposts rattle under his grip. But even a man like

Hafiz had his limits. He suddenly growled and grabbed Lacey's arms.

His kiss was hard and possessive. Her heart raced as the anticipation built deep inside her.

Hafiz tore his mouth away, and she tumbled down on to her back. She was sprawled naked before him. The ferocious hunger in his eyes made her shiver as the excitement clawed at her. She needed Hafiz, and she would go mad if she had to wait.

"Now," she demanded. She almost couldn't say the word, her chest aching as her heart pounded against her ribs. She rocked her hips as the desire coiled low in her pelvis.

Hafiz didn't argue. He grabbed the back of her legs and dragged her closer. Her stomach gave a nervous flip when she saw his harsh and intense expression.

After he wrapped her legs around his waist, Hafiz ruthlessly tilted her hips. She felt exposed. Wild and beautiful. Vulnerable and yet powerful.

Her heart stopped as he drove into her. Lacey

moaned as she yielded, arching her body to accept him. There was no finesse or sophistication. Her hips bucked to an ancient rhythm as she met his thrusts.

She wanted to hold on to this moment and make it last, but she couldn't tame the white heat that threatened to overpower her. Lacey closed her eyes and allowed the sensations to claim her as she cried out Hafiz's name.

Hours later, they lay together. Lacey's back was tucked against Hafiz's chest. Her long hair, tangled and damp with sweat, was pushed to the side as he placed a soft kiss on her neck. The blanket and sheets were in disarray on the floor, but Lacey didn't feel the need to warm their naked bodies. Hafiz's body heat was all she needed.

Lacey deliberately took an even breath and slowly exhaled. She wasn't going to cry. Not yet. She didn't want Hafiz's last memory of her to include that.

She focused her attention on their joined

hands, barely visible in the darkened room. She idly played with his hand, rubbing his palm and stroking the length of his fingers. Hafiz did the same, as if silently memorizing every inch of her hand.

They were so different, Lacey decided. Hafiz's hand was large and strong. Hers was more delicate. Her job as a pianist relied on her hands while Hafiz never used his for physical labor. His skin was golden and hers was ivory.

Her fingers clenched his. She stared at their clasped hands, noticing the soft shine of Hafiz's royal ring. She glanced at the window, her heart aching with knowing, when she saw the light filtering through the gap in the curtains.

The night had ended. Their time was over.

Lacey was reluctant to point it out. If Hafiz wasn't going to comment on it, why should she? After all, they didn't define when night ended. The people of Rudaynah didn't start the day until close to noon.

She knew she was grasping for more time. Lacey bit her lip as she watched Hafiz twist his fingers around hers. She wanted to grab his hands and hold them tight.

She was in danger of never letting him go.

Lacey glanced at the window again. They had not squeezed out every minute of their night together. How long had they spent gazing in each other's eyes, holding each other, not saying a word? But she wouldn't regret those quiet moments. They meant something to her. It made her feel connected to Hafiz.

Lacey swept the tip of her tongue along her bottom lip before she spoke. "It's morning."

Her voice shattered the peaceful silence. She felt the tension in Hafiz's muscles before his fingers gripped hers.

"No, it's not," Hafiz replied in his deep, rumbling voice as his warm breath wafted against her ear.

She frowned and motioned at the window. "It's sunrise."

"I disagree." Hafiz gently turned her so she lay on her back. "The sun is still rising. It isn't morning yet. We still have time."

He wasn't ready to end this, either. Lacey gazed lovingly at his face above hers. She brushed her fingertips along his jaw, the dark stubble rough against her skin.

"I love you, Hafiz."

A dark and bittersweet emotion she couldn't define flashed in his eyes. Hafiz slowly lowered his head and bestowed a gentle kiss on her lips.

She didn't move as he placed another soft kiss on her cheek and yet another on her brow. It was more than saying goodbye. He touched her with reverence.

She closed her eyes, desperate to hide her tears, as Hafiz cupped her face with care. He tipped her head back against the pillows and kissed her again. His mouth barely grazed hers.

Lacey wanted to capture his lips and deepen the kiss. But Hafiz slid his mouth to her chin before leaving a trail of kisses along her throat.

She swallowed hard as Hafiz darted his tongue at the dip of her collarbone before pressing his mouth against the pulse point at the base of her throat. She gasped as he suckled her skin between his sharp teeth and left his mark on her.

He didn't need to brand her. She was already his, and nothing—not time, not distance—would change that.

"Hafiz…" she said in a moan as she reached for him. He stopped her and wrapped his hands around her wrists before lowering her arms on the mattress.

"Shh," he whispered as he settled between her legs. He continued his path and kissed the slope of her breast. Lacey arched her spine as he teased her with his mouth.

Hafiz knew how to touch her, how to draw out the pleasure until it became torment. She hissed between her teeth as he laved his tongue against her tight nipple before drawing it into his hot mouth.

She fought against his hold, wanting to grab the back of his head, needing to hold him against her chest, but Hafiz didn't let go.

As sweat formed on her skin while she trembled with need, Hafiz silently continued his descent down her abdomen. Lust, hot and thick, flooded her pelvis. She rocked her hips insistently as Hafiz licked and nibbled and kissed her.

His path was slow, lazy and thorough. She glanced at the window. The sunlight was getting brighter and stronger.

Hafiz bent his head and pressed his mouth on her sex. Lacey moaned as she bucked against his tongue. He released her wrists to spread her legs wider. Lacey grabbed his head, bunching his short hair in her fists as he pleasured her.

She tried to hold back, wanting to make this last, but her climax was swift and sharp. She cried out as it consumed her. Her hips bucked wildly as she rode the sensations.

Her stomach clenched with anticipation as Hafiz slid his hands under her hips. His touch was urgent. She opened her eyes to see him tower over her. There was a primitive look in his eyes as he knelt between her legs.

She felt the rounded tip of his erection pressing against her. Hafiz entered her fully, and she groaned with deep satisfaction. She watched as he closed his eyes and tipped his head back as he struggled for the last of his control.

Lacey's flesh gripped him hard as she felt her body climbing fast toward another climax. She bucked against Hafiz, and he braced his arms next to her. He recaptured her hands and curled his fingers around hers.

"Hafiz…" she whimpered as he rested his forehead against hers. She went silent as he met her gaze. She allowed him to watch her every emotion and response flicker in her eyes. She hid nothing as she climaxed again, harder and longer.

And when her release triggered his, she didn't look away. Lacey let Hafiz know how much pleasure she received from watching him. She heard his hoarse cry before she closed her eyes, allowing exhaustion to claim her.

Lacey's eyes bolted open. The first thing she heard was the drone of the high-speed ceiling fan. Then she noticed the sheets tucked neatly around her body.

Panic crumbled on top of her. She jackknifed into a sitting position and looked at Hafiz's side of the bed. It was empty.

"No," she whispered. "Noooo." She pushed the sheets away as if he would suddenly appear.

She wildly looked around the room. She knew she'd asked for this night only, but she wished she had asked for more. Much more. Even if she knew it wasn't possible, she would have thrown her pride to the wind and begged for more time.

Lacey stumbled out of bed and grabbed for her robe. Hafiz's side of the bed was warm. There was a chance that he was still there.

"Hafiz?" she called out with a nervous tremble as she tied the sash of her robe. The silence taunted her. Biting down on her bottom lip, she opened the bedroom door. Hope leached from her bones as she stared into the empty drawing room.

Lacey slammed the door shut and ran to the window, her bare feet slapping against the floor.

She ripped the curtains to the side and searched the quiet streets.

Her heart lodged in her throat as she saw the familiar figure walking across the street.

For a brief moment, Lacey thought she was mistaken. The man didn't stride through the streets with regal arrogance. Hafiz walked slowly. Hesitantly. His head was bowed, his shoulder hunched.

She raised her fists, ready to beat at the glass and call for him to turn around.

Instinct stopped her. She knew it was hard for him to walk away. Probably just as difficult as it was to let him leave. She had to be strong. For him, if not for herself.

She pressed her forehead against the window, letting her fingers streak against the glass. "Hafiz..." she cried weakly.

Her eyes widened as she watched him slow to a halt. It was impossible for him to have heard her whimper. Hafiz turned slightly to the side and caught himself before glancing at her window.

Her heart pounded until she thought her ears would burst from the sound. She needed one more look. Just one more so she could carry it with her to ease her loneliness. She needed another look to remember that she was loved once.

But she also didn't want him to turn around. She needed him to be strong. She needed to see his strength and know that he was going to be okay. That he was going to stand alone as he had before he met her.

Lacey pressed her lips together, her breath suspended as Hafiz paused. Tears cascaded down her cheeks as she felt her future clinging to this moment.

Hafiz straightened his shoulders and resolutely turned away. Lacey felt shell-shocked. Her future took a free fall into the dark and desolate abyss.

It was a bittersweet sight for her to see Hafiz stride away. She stared at him, sobbing noisily until he turned the corner. Her gaze didn't move from the empty spot just in case he changed his mind. Her vision blurred and her eyes stung as she kept watch for the possibility that he needed to steal one more glance.

But it wasn't going to happen. He was strong enough for the both of them. The knowledge chipped away at her as she sank against the wall into an untidy heap.

It was over. They were no longer together.

Lacey felt as if she was going to splinter and die. And she had no idea how she was going to prevent falling apart without Hafiz holding her tight and giving a piece of his strength to her.

CHAPTER FIVE

HAFIZ REALIZED HE must have looked quite fierce by the way the office workers cowered when he strode in. *Too bad,* he thought as he cast a cold look at a young businessman who had the misfortune of being in his eyesight. Hafiz didn't feel like altering his expression.

Usually he looked forward to coming into his downtown office in the afternoon once he had met all of his royal duties for the day. It felt good to get out of the palace that was as quiet as a mausoleum. Although it had been built by his ancestors, the historical site—or the people inside it—didn't reflect who he was. The royal viziers were too concerned with protocol and tradition. They didn't like any new idea. Or any idea *he* had.

The royal court seemed to have forgotten that

he was brought up to serve and look after the sultanate. His education and experience had been focused on international relations and business. He had so many plans and initiatives to improve the lives of his countrymen, but no one wanted to listen to the prince who had fallen out of favor. That would change once he married the sultan's choice.

He strode to his desk and noted that, unlike his troubled mind, everything in his office was in order. The modern building, complete with state-of-the-art equipment, usually crackled with energy from dawn to dusk. The sultan and the palace had no say in what went on in these offices. Here Hafiz had the freedom to explore and take risks.

The young men he employed outside of the palace were unquestionably loyal, efficient and brilliant. They were men who were educated outside of Rudaynah, but returned home so they could make a difference. They spoke Arabic and English fluently, usually within the same sentence. They were comfortable in business suits and traditional Rudaynahi robes. Men very much like him, except for a few drops of royal blood and a few years in the world that had stripped away any idealism.

From the corner of his eye, Hafiz saw his executive secretary hurry toward him. One of the office assistants was already at his desk, trying to look invisible while carefully setting down a mug of coffee. The bitter scent was welcoming since he hadn't slept for days. Hafiz walked around his desk, determined to lose himself in his work.

"Good afternoon, Your Highness," the secretary said cautiously as he tugged at his silk tie. The man eyed him like he would a cobra ready to strike. "The changes in your schedule have been entered—"

Hafiz's attention immediately began to fade, which was unlike him. He was known for his focus and attention to detail, but he had been distracted for the past few days. Perhaps he was coming down with something. It had nothing to do with Lacey. He did not wallow in the past. He didn't focus on the things he couldn't change. He had moved on from Lacey.

Lacey. He refused to look at the window, but the pull was too great. Hafiz reluctantly looked outside, his gaze automatically seeking Lacey's penthouse apartment. A few months ago, he had picked the office building specifically for the view. He had found himself staring out of the window throughout the workdays, even though he knew he wouldn't catch a glimpse of Lacey. The knowledge that she was there always brought him peace. Until now.

The buzzing of his cell phone shattered his reverie. His gut twisted with anticipation and dread. Only a few people had this number. He grabbed the phone and looked at the caller ID. Disappointment crashed when he saw it wasn't Lacey. Hafiz dismissed his secretary with the wave of his hand and took the call.

"Your Highness? This is Glenn," Lacey's bodyguard quickly said to identify himself. "I'm sorry to call you, but we've hit a setback. Our exit visas have been delayed."

"Nothing works on time in Rudaynah." Hafiz rubbed his hand over his forehead and gave a short sigh of frustration. A sense of unease trickled down his spine. Was the palace behind this? Did they know about Lacey?

Hafiz discarded that thought. The palace wouldn't be concerned about an American nightclub singer. "Did they say why?"

"No. I bribed the right government officials, sat down and had tea at the chief of police's office, but I'm not getting any information."

Hafiz glanced out the window again. He had to get Lacey out before her presence could ruin everything he had worked toward. "Ordinarily I would have someone from the palace make a special request with the right official, but that would bring unwanted attention. We will have to wait it out. They should be ready in another day or two."

"Yes, sir."

"Would you please put Lacey on the phone, and I'll explain it to her." He shouldn't talk to Lacey. After all, they had said their goodbyes.

He wanted that night to be their last memory, but he also didn't want her to think he had abandoned her when she needed assistance.

There was a beat of silence, and Glenn cleared his throat. "Miss Maxwell is not here, sir."

"What?" Hafiz stared at Lacey's apartment. She had promised that she wouldn't venture out again. "Where is she?"

"She is at the Scimitar having tea with friends."

Hafiz's muscles jerked with surprise. *Friends? What friends?*

His gaze darted across the skyline to the luxurious hotel. The tall building was like a glass and metal spiral reaching out to the sun, reflecting the rays against the dark windows. "I don't understand."

"I apologize, sir. I would have accompanied her, but I was dealing with the exit visas. She had left before I got back."

Lacey had friends? Hafiz felt his frown deepen. Lacey had a world outside of the apartment. A world that didn't include him. He wasn't sure why he was so surprised. Lacey had a large group of friends in St. Louis.

But she never talked about these friends. That was strange. Lacey told him everything. Or he thought she did. Why had she been hiding this information?

"Who are these friends?" Hafiz asked tersely, interrupting Glenn's excuse. If one of them had a male name… Hafiz gritted his teeth and clenched his hand into a fist.

"No need to be concerned, sir," Glenn replied. "These women are above reproach. They are the wives of ambassadors and government ministers."

Hafiz went cold as he remained perfectly still. His ex-mistress was socializing with the most influential and powerful women of Rudaynah? The very mistress he broke up with so he could marry another? Hafiz slowly closed his eyes as the tension wrapped around his chest and squeezed. Glenn was incorrect. He had every reason to worry.

* * *

Lacey always thought the tearoom at the Scimitar was an unlikely mix of cultures. She stared at the plate that offered scones and slices of cinnamon date cake. A copper *cezve* for Turkish coffee sat next to an ornate silver teapot. A golden table runner with an intricate geometric design lay on top of the white linen tablecloth.

"You look so different in Western clothes," Inas told Lacey as she nibbled on a fried pastry ball that was dipped in a thick syrup. "I hardly recognized you."

"I feel different," Lacey admitted as she self-consciously tucked her hair behind her ear. She felt undressed wearing a simple green dress with long sleeves and a high neckline. Her makeup was minimal, and her shoes had a low heel. She was covered, but it didn't feel as if it was enough. "It's strange not wearing a caftan."

"Why the sudden change?" Janet, an ambassador's wife, asked as she patted a linen napkin to her bright red lips. Tall, blond and willowy, Janet had lived in the sultanate for years but chose not to wear the native clothes, no matter how warm the weather turned. "We're still in Rudaynah."

"I'm trying to get used to my old clothes," Lacey explained, but it wasn't the whole truth. When she'd first moved here, Lacey had originally chosen to wear the scarves and caftans, believing it was the first step to enter this world. Now she realized it had been a waste of time. "Although I really didn't fit in here."

"Nonsense." Inas flipped her long black braid over her shoulder. "You were one of my hardest-working students. So determined. If you had stayed here a little longer, I'm sure you would have become proficient in Arabic."

"Thank you." She had wanted to surprise Hafiz with her grasp of the language. One of her goals had been to watch his face soften when she declared her love in his native tongue.

"I don't know what our charity is going to do without you," Janet said with a sigh. "We made great strides once you joined. Are you sure you have to leave right away?"

"Yes, we need to move. It's urgent for my… uncle to get to his next work project." Part of her wished she could have left on the first flight out, but she was finding the idea of permanently leaving Hafiz very difficult. "We're just waiting for the exit visas."

"Those are just a formality," Inas insisted. "But if you're still going to be here this weekend, you must attend my daughter's wedding reception. The marriage contract ceremony is for family only, but the reception is going to be here for all of our friends. Oh, and you should see the dancers we hired for the *zaffa* procession!"

"I would like that." She had heard every detail about the upcoming wedding and wanted to be there to share her friend's special moment. But her moments with Hafiz had come first, and she had reluctantly declined because it would have interfered with her time with him.

What had Hafiz given up to spend time with her? Lacey frowned as the thought whispered into her mind. She shouldn't compare. Hafiz was a busy and important man.

"Most of the royal court will be there because my husband and the groom's father are government ministers. I know you couldn't attend before because your aunt and uncle had a previous engagement, but this will be the last time we see each other. Extend the invitation to them and…" Inas frowned when the quiet buzz of conversation suddenly died. She set down her teacup, her gold bracelets tinkling, as she looked over her shoulder. "What's happening?"

"I'm not sure," Janet murmured as she craned her neck. "Everyone is looking at the door to the lobby."

"Oh, my goodness," Inas whispered and turned to face her friends. Her eyes were wide with delight. "It's the prince."

Lacey flinched at her friend's announcement. Her heartbeat stuttered over the possibility of seeing Hafiz again. "Which one? Which prince?"

"The oldest. Hafiz."

Lacey struggled for her next breath when she saw Hafiz being escorted through the tearoom. He effortlessly commanded attention. It wasn't because the aggressive lines of his dark business suit emphasized his muscular body, or the haughty jut of his chin. It wasn't because he walked like a conqueror or because of his royal status. It was because he exuded a power that indicated that he was a valuable ally or a dangerous opponent. This was someone who could ruin a man's life with the snap of his fingers or steal a woman's heart with a smile.

Hafiz strode past her, never meeting her startled gaze. His face was rigid, as if it had been hewn from stone.

He didn't see her. Lacey's lips parted as she stared after him. How was that possible? She would always capture his gaze the moment she walked into the room.

A thousand petty emotions burst and crawled under her skin. She wouldn't give in to them. She shouldn't care that she was invisible three days after he left her. She expected it. That would have always been her status in public had she stayed with Hafiz.

And she didn't want a life like that, Lacey reminded herself, closing her eyes and drawing the last of her composure. She didn't want to come in second, even if it meant a life without Hafiz. She refused to be on the side. She wouldn't be an afterthought again.

"He's gorgeous," Janet said in a low voice as they watched Hafiz stride out of the tearoom to what she suspected was the private dining areas.

"So is his fiancée," Inas informed them. "I know the Abdullah family."

Lacey winced. She wished she hadn't heard that. She didn't want to know anything about the woman who got to marry Hafiz. It was easier for her that way.

Janet leaned forward. "What is she like?"

"Nabeela is the perfect Rudaynahi woman."

Lacey's muscles locked. Now she had a name to go with the woman. Somehow that made it worse. She didn't want to put a name or a face to the person who got the man she loved.

"She has been groomed for life at the palace. Her parents were hoping she would marry a royal adviser or minister. They never thought the sultan and his wife would choose her to become a princess. She'll make a good wife for Hafiz."

No, she won't. He's mine. The thought savagely swiped at her like a claw. It tore at the thin façade she'd carefully constructed after finding out about Hafiz's wedding, exposing the truth that bled underneath. It punctured the festering pain she tried to ignore.

She knew Hafiz was going to be married, but she didn't allow herself to think past the wedding. She thought of Nabeela as the bride. She'd never thought of them as a couple. As partners. As husband and wife.

Lacey looked down hurriedly, the table weaving and buckling before her eyes. The knowledge made her physically ill. She knew it wasn't a love match, but it didn't stop the bilious green ribbons of jealousy snaking around her heart.

Her poisonous emotions ate away at her until she felt like a brittle, hollowed-out shell. A series of primal responses, each sharper than the previous one, battered her mind, her heart and her pride.

"Well, I heard it's not Nabeela's beauty that made Prince Hafiz accept," Janet said in a sly tone.

Lacey wanted to change the topic immediately. But she was scared to open her mouth, not sure if her secrets or a scream of howling pain would spill out. She stared at her teacup and forced herself to reach for it. She didn't like how her hands trembled.

"Rumor has it that the sultan and the prince made an agreement," Janet whispered fiercely. "If he marries this Nabeela without incident, Hafiz will become the crown prince."

Lacey's breath hitched in her throat. She set the cup down before it snapped in her hands.

So that was the reason. It made sense, and she didn't question it.

Lacey sank back in her plush chair and tilted her head up. She stared at the mosaic ceiling made of lapis lazuli as the low murmur of different languages faded into a hum. The clink of fine china blurred into nothing as her thoughts spun wildly.

She always knew Hafiz was ambitious. Driven and determined. A man like Hafiz couldn't give up the chance of the throne. Even if it meant discarding his mistress. Although now she wondered if it had been a difficult decision for him. She couldn't compete with a crown.

She should have seen the signs. After all, she had been in this position before. Her parents had been just as driven, just as single-minded with their dreams to become rich and famous. Once they decided having a child was holding them back, they had abandoned her with a swiftness that still took her breath away.

But this time she hadn't looked for signs because she thought they were in love. She had wanted to believe that this time she wasn't the burden. That she was not only welcomed into Hafiz's life, but that he would move heaven and earth to be with her.

When was she going to learn? She did not inspire that kind of devotion. No one would ever love her like that.

"What about his brother?" Lacey's voice sounded rough to her ears. She pushed her plate away with tense fingers. "I thought he was the crown prince."

"Ashraf?" Janet asked. "Yes, I wonder how he feels about this new development. He's been the heir to the throne for a decade."

"A decade?" Lacey repeated slowly. "How old is he?"

"Just a few years younger than Prince Hafiz," Janet said, glancing at Inas for confirmation. "He became the heir to the throne when Hafiz lost his birthright."

Lacey blinked slowly as a buzzing sound grew in her ears. "Hafiz lost—?" She gripped the edge of the table as her heart fluttered against her rib cage. "I mean…*Prince* Hafiz? What do you mean by birthright?"

"He was in line to be the next sultan," Janet explained.

Lacey tilted her head sharply. Her arms went lax as she slumped in her chair. She felt as if she was missing a vital piece of information. "He was *supposed* to inherit the throne? When did this happen?"

"How do you not know this?" Inas's eyes widened as she leaned over the table. "I thought we covered this during your history lessons."

Lacey slowly shook her head. "How can a prince be displaced in the line of succession?" She was hesitant to even ask. Did he renounce his right? Did he commit a heinous crime? Neither sounded like something Hafiz would do. "You have to do something really bad, right?"

"I don't have all the details on that, but I can tell you this." Inas gave a cautious glance at the tables surrounding them before she went on. "It had something to do with a woman."

Lacey felt her lungs shrivel up as the bitter

taste of despair filled her mouth. Hafiz lost everything over a woman? Numbness invaded her bones, protecting her before she doubled over from the intense pain.

"What woman?" Lacey asked dully. She must have been extraordinary for Hafiz to take such a risk. It didn't make sense. The man would do anything to protect and serve his country. He did not put anyone before his duty. Hafiz did not put *himself* before Rudaynah.

"I heard it was a mistress," Janet said quietly. "A series of mistresses."

Inas shrugged. "One woman is all that it would take to lose the throne."

A mistress. No, *mistresses*. She shouldn't be surprised. Hafiz was incredibly sophisticated and knowledgeable in the bedroom. Yet for some reason she felt as if her role in his life was different from all the other women. That she was somehow special.

Maybe she was special. Maybe... Lacey clenched her hands together under the table.

She should stop trying to make her relationship with Hafiz into a fairy tale.

But why had he risked everything again by bringing her to his sultanate? By starting the relationship in the first place? What provoked him to flaunt authority and break the rules again?

Again? There was no indication that he went without a mistress after he lost his right to the throne. Lacey went cold. Was bringing his mistress to the sultanate something he did often? Did he get a new model every year? Lacey slowly closed her eyes. Her jaw trembled as the hot tears stung her eyes.

She needed to figure out what was going on. She wanted to go home, lock herself in her room and curl up in a ball to ward off the anguish that was crashing against her in waves. But first she had to leave the tearoom before she embarrassed herself.

Lacey opened her eyes and kept her head down before anyone saw her distress. "Oh, look at the time!" she said as she barely glanced at her wristwatch. "I didn't realize it was so late."

Her movements felt awkward as she rose from the table and said goodbye to her friends. The flurry of hugs and promises did nothing to calm her. Her heart pumped fast as she struggled with the information about Hafiz's past.

She turned and saw one of the hotel bellmen standing in front of her. His blue uniform was the same color as the mosaic ceiling. "Miss Maxwell? Are you leaving?" the young man asked. "A Mr. Glenn called for you. He says it's urgent."

"Oh!" She clumsily patted her purse and realized she didn't bring her cell phone because it hadn't been charged due to another power outage. "Is there a phone I can use?"

"Please follow me to one of the conference rooms, and you may contact him in private."

"Thank you." She hurried after the bellman, her legs unsteady after the surprise she had received. She felt dizzy, as if her world had been knocked off its axis. Lacey was out of breath by the time she reached the conference room. She managed to give the man a simple nod as he opened the door with a flourish.

She stepped inside the long room and felt the door close behind her. The conference room was intimidating with its heavy furniture and arched ceilings. The thick blue curtains were pulled shut, and the silence was oppressive.

Lacey frowned when she noticed there was no phone on the oversized conference table. She inhaled the familiar scent of sandalwood that never failed to stir a deep craving inside her.

Hafiz.

It was her only warning before her spine was pressed up against the wall.

Strong arms bracketed her head. Hafiz's broad shoulders were encased in an expensive suit jacket. She wanted to cling on to them. She looked up and saw that Hafiz's face loomed above hers.

He was just a kiss away. After convincing herself that she would never be able to touch him, having him so close was overwhelming. She leaned forward as her eyelashes drifted shut.

"What the hell are you up to, Lacey?" Hafiz asked through clenched teeth.

CHAPTER SIX

SHE STIFFENED AND her lashes fluttered. Hafiz's brown eyes shone with cold anger. Lacey's stomach quavered at his ferocious look. It was not the kind of greeting one lover gave to another.

But then, they weren't lovers anymore. Any momentary fantasy she harbored broke like crackling ice. They might have been alone in the room, but they were not together. They were acquaintances. Their past was erased as if it never existed. She needed to remember that.

She rested heavily against the wall as if it was the only thing in the room that seemed to be able to support her. She tilted her chin and looked directly at Hafiz. "Good afternoon to you, too, Your Highness," she replied as tears pushed against the backs of her eyes.

"Lacey," he bit out. "I want an answer."

She pressed her lips together and dug her fingers against her purse. Lacey wished she could turn off her emotions with the same effortlessness as Hafiz. She wished his cool treatment didn't feel like a slap in the face.

She looked away and wrapped her arms around her middle. She couldn't handle the lack of intimacy in his dark eyes. She already missed the aura of shared secrets that cocooned them for a year.

She felt as if she was being tugged into a sandstorm and had nothing to hold on to. She could only rely on herself. It had always been that way. When she first met Hafiz, she thought she wouldn't be so alone in the world. Now she understood that it had been an illusion.

"I was having tea with a couple of my friends," she said, hating how her voice cracked.

"Why is this the first I've heard about these so-called friends?"

"You never asked." Lacey felt the flare of anger. "You never asked about my day or how

I was coping living in this country." The anger burned hotter, and she ducked under his arm and walked away. "You just assumed I spent every waking moment in my apartment. Did you think I powered down until you returned?"

"If you wanted to share something, there was nothing and no one holding you back." Hafiz's eyes narrowed as he watched her move to one end of the table. "Why am I hearing about this now?"

She shrugged. Some of it was her fault. She was reacting in the same way as when she had felt her parents' interest slipping. She'd known if she wanted to retain Hafiz's attention, have him keep coming back, she needed to be positive. She had to be entertaining, and put all of the focus on him. If she had been too needy, he would start to distance himself.

"How is someone like you friends with an ambassador's wife? Or the wife of a deputy minister?"

Lacey raised her eyebrow and met his gaze.

She would not show how much those words hurt. "Someone like me?"

"You know what I mean." Hafiz rubbed the back of his neck with impatience. "You don't share the same status or have the same interests."

"So, what you're really asking is how a mistress became friends with respectable women?" she asked in a cool tone.

"Yes." Hafiz crossed his arms. "That's exactly what I'm saying."

The room tilted sickeningly for a moment. Did he know what he was saying? Did he care? She closed her eyes and swallowed. "You do realize that you're the one who made me a mistress."

"And you accepted the offer."

His indifference cut like a knife. A sarcastic rejoinder danced on her tongue like a hot pepper.

"Why are you friends with these women," he asked, "and why did you meet with them today?"

"Do you know why I play the piano?" Lacey

asked as she pulled out a chair and sat down at the head of the table.

Hafiz gave her an incredulous look and spread his arms out wide. "What does this have to do with the women you were with?"

"A lot of people think I play piano because I grew up in a musical environment," Lacey continued as if he hadn't spoken. "My parents are musicians, so, therefore, I must have their interests rub off on me."

Hafiz leaned his shoulder against the wall. "Get to the point, Lacey."

"My parents didn't care if I took up a musical instrument or not. I thought that if I learned how to play the piano, and played exceptionally well, I could be part of their lives. They would take me on the road with them and I wouldn't be left behind all the time."

"And?"

The corner of her mouth twitched as she remembered her parents' harsh and immediate rejection to that plan. How her father had declared that one of the benefits of the road trips was taking a break from being parents. "It didn't work. But for some reason, I thought it would work this time."

Hafiz frowned. "This time?"

"When you invited me to live here, I thought we were building toward a future. A life together." She hastily looked away. She was embarrassed by her ignorance, her belief that they would live happily ever after. "And I worked to make this my new home. Inas is very proud of her heritage and she used to be a teacher. She's been my Arabic and history tutor."

"You've been learning Arabic? I've never heard you speak it."

She saw the deep suspicion in his eyes and a dull ache of disappointment spread through her chest. "I wasn't ready to show off my language skills just yet. I'm nowhere near fluent."

His mouth twisted, and she knew he didn't believe her. "And the ambassador's wife?"

"I met Janet at her charity against hunger. We've been working together for the past six months." Her voice trailed off when she noticed that she was following the same pattern and getting the same results.

Both times she had placed all of her energy into another person's interest. Both times she had thought the commitment would pay off. That they would see how she fit seamlessly into their world and welcome her with open arms. At the very least, appreciate her efforts.

It shouldn't be this hard to keep her loved ones in her life. She had to stop giving her all to people who didn't want it. Didn't want her.

"And you just happen to become friends." Hafiz's voice broke through her thoughts. "With the two women who could destroy everything I've worked for if they mention a rumor to one of their powerful friends or husbands."

"Is that what you're worried about?" Lacey began to tap her fingers on the table. "In all our time together, I've never done anything to hurt you. Why would you think I'd do that now?"

"Because you thought I would marry you one day, and instead I'm marrying someone else. You want revenge."

"Wait a minute! Are you saying—" She sat up straight and pressed her hands against her chest. "Do you think I'm trying to—"

He speared her with an icy cold glare. "Hell hath no fury like a woman scorned."

"Scorned woman? You've scorned me? No, you've sacrificed me, but—"

"And you needed to hit me back." He widened his arms as if offering her another shot.

"You think I have the power to hurt you?" she asked through barely parted lips. She realized that she did have that power, temporarily. "That's why you didn't tell me. I never thought you were a coward. And you aren't. You just don't give information unless it's in your interest."

She bit the inside of her lip as he walked to her, his stride reminding her of a stalking panther.

"Explain yourself, Lacey," he said softly with just a bite of warning.

"The agreement between you and the sultan," she said hurriedly. "The one about you becoming the crown prince if you marry his choice of bride."

Surprise flashed in his dark eyes before he placed his fists on his lean hips. "How do you know about that?"

Lacey dipped her head as the last glimmer of hope faded. So it was true. He gave her up for a chance to become the next sultan. "Everyone knows."

"The agreement came after I was engaged," he said stiffly before he turned around. "I don't know why I'm explaining this to you."

You mean, to someone like you, Lacey silently added. "Do you want to be the sultan?"

Hafiz's shoulders grew rigid as he turned around. "Of course. I know I can do the job. For the past ten years, I've worked hard to prove it to others."

"Don't you want to do something different?" she asked.

"Why would I give up this opportunity?"

Why would he, other than to have a life that would include her? It wasn't worth the sacrifice. And he supposedly made the decision to end their relationship *before* the sultan's offer.

"Look at the impact you've made on your own," she pointed out. "Think of what else you could do without the interference of the palace."

"You don't understand, Lacey," he said wearily as he thrust his fingers in his dark hair. "I was born for this. It's my destiny."

"I know. It's why you push yourself." Her toe tapped a nervous staccato beat before she dove into uncharted territory. "It's not out of ambition, is it? You're looking for redemption."

He tilted his head as if he was scenting danger. As if she was getting too close to his secret. Too close to the truth.

"You lost your birthright ten years ago. That's why your brother was chosen over you. And you've been trying to get it back."

She knew the truth. Shame swept through Hafiz. It burned through his veins, and he instinctively hunched his shoulders to ward it off.

He looked at the floor, unable to meet her eyes, even though she had the right to judge him. "How do you know about that?" he asked hoarsely.

The tapping of her toe halted. The silence vibrated around him. "I wish I had heard it from you."

Hafiz said nothing. He wished he could have denied it, but he'd withstood the disgrace for nearly a decade. It should be no different now.

But it was. He didn't want Lacey to know about his mistakes. About the person he used to be.

Lacey was the first to break the silence. "Why didn't you tell me?"

Because he was a better person when he was with Lacey. He could be the man he wanted to be, the prince he strived to become for his country. She believed he could do the impossible, and he knew he could with her by his side. Had she known about his past, would she still have believed? He knew she wouldn't.

But Lacey knew now. And her opinion meant

the most to him. He didn't know how he would stand up against her disillusionment. "It's not something I'm proud of."

"So you hid it from me?" she asked. He heard the anger wobbling in her voice. "You only showed me one side of you? I thought we had been closer than that."

Hafiz pulled open a curtain and let the bright sunlight stream in the dark room. The image of his beloved country didn't soothe the twinge inside him. He was drowning in regret and there was no hope of escape.

He bunched his hands into tight fist, imagining the relief if he punched through the glass. He could hear the shattering window in his mind, but he wouldn't act on the impulse. But, oh, what he wouldn't do to get out of this room… away from Lacey's steady gaze.

"You were just a teenager when you lost your title as crown prince?"

"No, I was an adult. I was twenty-one." Hafiz had a feeling that was the easiest question he would be facing from Lacey.

"Really?" She made a sympathetic cluck with her tongue. "That's harsh. Being twenty-one is all about pushing the limits. Pushing boundaries."

He shook his head. It should have warmed his heart that Lacey automatically defended him, but he knew it wasn't going to last. "It's different for me."

"Because you're a prince? The heir to the throne?"

"Because my country came into a great deal of wealth when I was eighteen. I was sent to the States to get an education. To learn how to protect and grow the wealth." He took a deep breath and turned to face her. "Instead I spent it."

Her eyes widened as her mouth open and shut. "All of it?" she croaked out.

"No. It doesn't matter how many millions I spent." The amount was branded into his soul for eternity, but the numbers could never convey the suffering of others. "I spent it. I stole it." He still flinched at the stripped-down version of his action. "I stole the money from the people of Rudaynah for my own pleasure. I was the playboy prince the tabloids love to hate."

Lacey stared at him as if he was a stranger to her. It was better than looking at him with the disgust he felt for himself. "That doesn't sound like you at all."

"It was me," he said brutally. "Look it up. The sultan tried to hide the story, but you can find it if you look hard enough. My spending habits had been legendary," he said, humility threading his voice.

"What stopped it?"

"The sultan received reports and called me home. The moment I returned I saw how Rudaynah had yet to see any progress. It humbled me. Shamed me more than any lecture or punishment."

Lacey frowned. "And your punishment for spending the money was losing your right to the throne?"

"No. I was stripped of any responsibility or authority. Of any rights or privileges. I was spared getting lashes because of my royal status. I didn't leave Rudaynah until I could regain my father's trust. And I still didn't leave the borders until I felt it was necessary."

"But that doesn't explain to me how you lost your birthright."

The punishment he'd received was paltry considering his crime, but the sultan didn't want people to know the whole story. "One of the reports the sultan received had to do with my mistress at the time."

"I see," she said stiffly.

"You don't see." He looked directly in her blue eyes and braced himself. "My mistress became pregnant."

Lacey turned pale, but she regained her composure. "Is it yours?" she asked brusquely.

"I found out too late that she had an abortion," Hafiz said, the bitterness corroding inside him. "I've often wondered if the sultan campaigned for and funded it. Not directly, of course," he added cynically.

"I still don't understand—"

"Don't you get it, Lacey?" he barked out. "I couldn't uphold the expectations placed on me. I proved I wasn't leadership material." The list of his sins bore down on him. "I used the money for my own pleasure. I couldn't make my country proud. I couldn't provide the security of giving a rightful heir to the throne. But most of all, I couldn't protect my unborn child."

"Hafiz," Lacey said grimly as she walked toward him. He braced himself for her to launch into a tirade. For a stinging slap. It wouldn't hurt nearly as much as her disappointment.

She surprised him by placing a gentle hand on his arm. He looked down at her, bemused by the sincerity gleaming in her eyes. "Don't let your mistakes define you. You are a good man."

He drew back. She still believed in him. How could she? Wasn't she listening? "You're biased, but thanks."

"Give me some credit. I wouldn't give up everything familiar for a playboy prince. I certainly wouldn't follow any man to the ends of the earth."

"I believe the term you're looking for is 'this hell'," he reminded her.

Lacey looked chagrined but wouldn't be deterred. "And Rudaynah needs you. The mistake you made will serve you well." She paused, obviously searching for the right words. "You have risen from your past like…a phoenix from the ashes. You're stronger and smarter. You have worked hard all these years to take care of your countrymen."

But he would never regain the trust of the people. His brother kept his distance, as if poor judgment was contagious. His own parents couldn't stand the sight of him.

"I am not the kind of man you're trying to make me out to be." But he wanted to be. He wanted to deserve her admiration.

"You're good for Rudaynah. This sultanate needs you," Lacey insisted and cupped his face with her hand. "If I thought otherwise, I would take you away with me."

Hafiz leaned into her touch just as his cell phone rang. They both jumped as the harsh sound echoed in the cavernous room.

"Don't answer it," Lacey whispered.

"It would be Glenn. He would only call if it was important." He reached for the phone and answered it. "Yes?"

"Our exit visas have been denied," Glenn said.

A coldness settled inside Hafiz as he considered what that could mean. "Did they give a reason?"

"No, but they were acting strange. As if it hasn't happened before. What do you want me to do next, Your Highness?"

"Let me get back to you." Hafiz ended the call and pressed the phone against his chin as he stared out the window. He quickly analyzed the sultan's latest move and what it represented. He didn't like any of the answers.

"Is something wrong?" Lacey asked.

"Your exit visas have been denied," he murmured as he considered his next move.

"I thought the process was just a formality."

Lacey gasped, and she clapped her hand over her mouth. "Your father knows about me. He knows I'm your mistress."

"Let's not jump to conclusions. It could be a clerical error." Hafiz wanted to calm Lacey, but he knew his answer wouldn't soothe her.

"This doesn't make sense. Why can't I leave the country? Wouldn't your father give me the red carpet treatment to the first car out of here?"

"Not necessarily," Hafiz replied grimly.

Lacey pressed her lips together. "What's going on?"

"There's a possibility," he said, emphasizing the word, "that the sultan sees your presence as an advantage to him. It would make me the most agreeable groom."

"I don't like the sounds of that," Lacey said. "Am I in trouble? Is he going to use me to get to you?"

"I should have predicted it," Hafiz muttered. "The sultan had done this before."

"When? Ten years ago?" Lacey took a deep breath. "Hafiz, I need to know. What happened to your last mistress? The one who got pregnant?"

CHAPTER SEVEN

HAFIZ LEANED AGAINST the windowpane and closed his eyes as the guilt swamped him. He never forgot that time in his life, and he refused to forgive himself. The actions he took, the mistakes he made were part of him and had influenced his decisions to this day. And yet, he tried not to look too closely and inspect his flaws.

"Her name was Elizabeth," he said quietly. "I had already earned my reputation as the playboy prince when I met her in Monte Carlo."

"What was she like?" Lacey asked.

"Beautiful. Professional. Ambitious."

Lacey frowned. "You make her sound cold and unfeeling."

What he had shared with Elizabeth had nothing to do with warmth and affection. "She made her way through life as a mistress. Our relationship had been purely physical, and we both wanted it that way."

Because he hadn't been interested in romance or commitment. He had been too busy partying, gambling and exploring the world outside of Rudaynah and royal life.

Hafiz forced himself to continue. He knew Lacey needed to hear this. "We had only been together for a few months when I found out she was pregnant." Hafiz looked away. "I didn't handle the news well. I wish I could take back that moment and react differently."

"What did you do?" Lacey asked.

He didn't want to give a voice to the memories that haunted him. The moments that had demonstrated what kind of man he had been. Only he hadn't acted like a man.

"I was furious. Scared," he admitted with a sigh. "I knew that a baby was going to change everything. I swore the baby couldn't possibly be mine. I didn't *want* it to be mine."

Lacey rested her hand against his shoulder. "I can't imagine you acting like that, Hafiz."

"It was me. A spoiled and selfish prince who knew his freedom was about to be taken away from him. I accused Elizabeth of being unfaithful. I wasn't going to let her trap me or extort money from me." Hafiz raked his hand through his hair. "I hate the way I treated her."

"That may have been your first reaction, but I'm sure you saw reason once you calmed down."

Hafiz shook his head. Lacey thought too highly of him. He slowly turned around and faced her. "I left Elizabeth," he said, watching the surprise in Lacey's eyes. He hunched his shoulders as the remorse weighed heavily on him. "My father had demanded that I return home, and I used that as a way to hide from my responsibilities."

Lacey stared at him in disbelief. "You wouldn't do that."

"That was the lowest time of my life. I was trying to hide what I had done and conceal the person I was. Hide everything from the sultan and my countrymen. At times, I tried to hide the truth from myself."

"Impossible."

"It wasn't that hard to do. I wanted to convince myself that Elizabeth was the villain. I believed she tried to trick me and that she got what she deserved for attempting to get her claws into a prince."

"When did you decide she was not the villain?"

"It wasn't just one event. I started seeing how I treated everyone during that time. I should have treated her better. I had cut off all contact. And somehow I had convinced myself that I did the right thing."

"Did you try to find her after that and make it right?"

He nodded. "I wasn't able to travel, but I wasn't going to let it stop me. I was done making excuses. I had one of my representatives track her down." Hafiz took a deep breath. "But I was too late. Elizabeth had gotten an abortion."

The silence permeated the room as Hafiz

remembered getting that call. He had shattered from the grief. He had never been the same man after knowing he hadn't protected and provided for his unborn son.

"I was furious at myself," Hafiz said quietly. "If I had shown Elizabeth any concern or any sign that she could depend on me, she wouldn't have taken extreme measures."

"And you think your father was behind that?"

"I'm sure of it. Elizabeth had hinted it to my representative, but I think she was too afraid to speak plainly. She was afraid to cross the sultan, with good reason."

"Should I be afraid?"

"No," Hafiz said. "You can depend on me. I will not abandon you."

Lacey moved closer to him until her hip brushed against his. "I'm sorry. I'm sorry that my presence in your life is causing so many problems." The air around them pulsed with energy, but Hafiz didn't reach out for her. His fingers flexed, but his hands stayed by his side.

"You're not a burden," he said gruffly. Having Lacey in his life had been a gift.

Lacey leaned forward and pressed her forehead against his shoulder. Hafiz tensed and remained where he stood. It was still a risk. If someone walked into this room and saw him alone with Lacey…he didn't want to think about the consequences.

Hafiz cleared his throat and took a step away from her. "I have to go. I know how to fix this."

"What are you going to do?" she called after him as he strode to the door.

He set his mouth into a grim line. "Whatever it takes."

"This wedding reception is one of the most lavish I've seen. I don't know how Inas and her husband paid for it," Janet said a few days later as they slowly made their way through the crowded ballroom to the buffet. "I can't wait to eat."

"Where are the men?" Lacey asked. The ballroom was packed with women. Bright, garish colors swirled around Lacey and her friend Janet as the conversations swelled to an earsplitting decibel. Heavy perfumes of every imaginable flower clashed against one another.

"They are in the ballroom across the hall having their party," Janet informed her. "The men and women in Rudaynah don't celebrate together. This way the women can literally let their hair down and dance."

Lacey glanced at the stage where the bride sat. It seemed strange to Lacey that the newlywed couple would spend their wedding reception apart. Did it signify what was yet to come? That the marriage meant separate paths, separate lives, for the couple? Was this what all marriages were like in this country?

She studied the group of relatives on the stage surrounding the bride. "I still don't see Inas."

"We'll find her. By the way, I love what you're wearing. I thought you had given up wearing the traditional caftan."

"Thank you." Lacey glanced down at her pale blue caftan. She hadn't been certain about the transparent sleeves or the modest neckline. The skirt flared out gently, and the intricate embroidery design that ran down the front of the caftan matched her slippers. "I wanted one chance to wear it before I leave."

"Did you get your exit visas sorted out?"

"Uh...yes," she lied. "I'll be leaving very soon." As in tonight. But she couldn't let anyone know that.

She glanced at her jeweled watch and winced. The wedding reception had started late, and she should have returned home by now and gathered her things.

"Janet, why don't you go on ahead to the buffet? I have to leave."

"Already?" She shook her head. "You're going to miss the professional dancers and the wedding march. Not to mention the food!"

"I know, but I'm glad I had a chance to be here. I just hope leaving early doesn't offend Inas."

"She'll understand," Janet said as she hugged

Lacey goodbye. "You'll probably find her near the door greeting all the guests."

Lacey fought her way through the cluster of women. She couldn't help but wonder if Hafiz's wedding reception would be like this. She pushed the thought aside. She wasn't going to torture herself imagining what Hafiz's wedding to another woman was going to be like.

Lacey saw her friend near the entrance. "Inas!" She waved and hurried to greet the mother of the bride. "Inas, this wedding is beautiful. And your daughter!" She glanced at the woman on stage in the back of the ballroom. The young woman wore an embroidered red gown and veil. Heavy gold jewelry hung from her wrists and throat. "She looks like a princess."

"Lacey, I'm so happy to see you." Inas gave her a kiss on each cheek. "And you wouldn't believe who is here!"

The woman almost squealed. Lacey couldn't imagine who would cause this level of excitement. "Who?"

"Inas?" An older woman's voice wafted over

them. Inas's demeanor changed rapidly. Her smile widened, and she trembled with exhilaration. Inas struggled to lower her eyes as she gave a curtsey to the woman. She folded her hands neatly in front of her as she spoke respectfully in Arabic.

Lacey took a step back. Her instincts told her to melt into the crowd and disappear.

"Allow me to introduce you," Inas said as she grasped Lacey's elbow and brought her forward. Lacey stared at the older woman who wore a white scarf over her gray hair and a brocade caftan that concealed her body.

"Your Majesty, this is Lacey Maxwell. I tutored her in Arabic while she was visiting our sultanate. Lacey, this is the Sultana Zafirah of Rudaynah."

And Hafiz's mother. Lacey's knees buckled, and she quickly covered it up with a shaky curtsey.

She glanced at the sultana through her lashes and found the older woman inspecting her like a mangled insect carcass. It took every ounce of willpower for Lacey not to meet the woman's gaze. *This was probably why Hafiz didn't want you to meet his family.*

Lacey covertly looked at the exit and wondered how she was going to extract herself from this situation. Her mind went blank as panic congealed in her throat. "I understand one of your sons will be married soon," Lacey said in what she hoped was a respectful tone. "Congratulations."

The sultana stiffened, and Lacey wondered if she had broken some protocol. "Thank you," Sultana Zafirah said with a sniff.

Lacey hesitated, uncertain how to proceed. "I'm sure Miss Abdullah will be a worthy addition to your family."

The sultana gave a careless shrug. "More worthy than my son."

A startled gasp quickly evaporated in Lacey's throat as indignation mushroomed inside her chest. How dare the sultana say that about Hafiz? Lacey was stunned that the woman would say it to a stranger. There was no telling what was said in private.

Lacey looked away and fought back her words. Didn't Sultana Zafirah see how much her son worked and sacrificed to correct his mistakes? Didn't she care that he strove to become worthy, all the while knowing he would never reach his goal? Or was the sultana unwilling to recognize what her son has already achieved?

Tears smarted Lacey's eyes as hope shriveled up inside her. Why did Hafiz want to be with his family instead of her? The idea alone was like a knife sliding between her ribs before it gave a vicious twist. Was this what he really wanted?

How could she leave Hafiz here to face this alone? But deep down, she knew she wasn't an ally. She was a liability. She was going to leave so Hafiz could become the man he wanted to be. She wanted Rudaynah to benefit from his ideas and leadership, and she wanted the people to recognize his worth and abilities.

On a purely selfish level, she wanted her sacrifice to mean something. She wanted it be worth the pain, if that was possible.

The ballroom suddenly plunged into darkness. The initial squeals from the crowd turned into groans of people who were used to power outages. Lacey blinked wildly as the darkness shrouded her. She could already feel the difference in temperature as the air conditioner silenced.

"Nothing to worry about, Miss Maxwell." Sultana Zafirah said. The royal entourage bumped Lacey as they quickly surrounded the sultana. "The generator will turn on soon."

"Yes, Your Majesty."

The emergency lights gradually came on, casting an eerie green over the wedding guests. Just as everyone cheered, the lights blinked and flared before shutting off.

"No, no, no." Inas said. "This cannot happen at my daughter's wedding."

"I'll go see if there are any lights on in the hotel," Lacey offered. Sensing she only had a

few minutes before the lights and power returned, she slowly retreated.

Using the flurry of activity to her advantage,
Lacey turned around and made her way to the
exit. Her hands brushed against the heavy metal
door. She wrenched the handle, opening the
door a crack, and found the hallway was just
as dark as the ballroom. The moment she passed
the threshold, she breathed a sigh of relief.

As much as she wanted to celebrate her
friend's special moment, she found the business of marriage in Rudaynah too depressing.
It wasn't a union of two hearts as much as it
was a business alliance. The combining of two
families and two properties.

The lights came back on, and she heard the
murmurs of delight from the ballroom. Lacey
hurried down the steps to the main lobby when
she saw a familiar figure in a gray pinstripe suit
waiting at the bottom of the stairs.

"Where have you been?" Hafiz asked, glancing at his wristwatch. "We were supposed to
meet at your apartment."

"Hafiz?" She remembered that the sultana and the most influential people in the country were in the next room. He was placing himself at risk. "You can't be here. It's too dangerous. Your—"

"I'm fully aware of it," Hafiz said as he fell into step with her. "If you want to get to Abu Dhabi tonight, we must leave now."

"I'm sorry I'm late. I'm never late."

Hafiz set his mouth in a grim line. "My limousine is waiting right outside the entrance. Once we leave, then we will discuss what you were doing with my mother."

Lacey stiffened as she heard the accusation in his tone. How did he find out about that? She didn't have to see Hafiz's face to know he was angry. But why was he blaming her?

"I didn't know the sultana was going to make an appearance. How would I?"

Hafiz muttered something succinct as he ushered her out the hotel. Guilt slammed through her. She didn't want to be a hindrance. She hated being the cause of his troubles.

Lacey paused. She wasn't a hindrance. She wasn't a liability. The only thing she was guilty of was loving a man who didn't think she was good enough to marry.

CHAPTER EIGHT

HAFIZ KEPT HIS anger in check as he got into the waiting limousine. Tonight he had to send away the one person who mattered the most to him. He wanted to rage against the world, destroy everything around him and allow the fury to consume him. Instead he closed the car door with deliberate care.

The car jerked into full speed. He barely glanced at Lacey sitting regally on the other side of the back seat. He didn't trust himself to speak or look at her.

What was it about this woman? Did she trigger a self-destructive tendency in him? Why had he been willing to risk everything for Lacey? What made him lower his guard when they had been in danger of discovery? Why couldn't he have fallen for someone who would make his life easier?

"I have nothing to say." Lacey stared straight ahead. "I did nothing wrong."

He sliced his hand in the air. "Yes, you did," he replied in a low growl. In the past Lacey's hurt would have destroyed him until he did everything in his power to make her happy, but at the moment he wished she would see the world through his eyes.

"I don't have to explain myself," Lacey continued. "My friend introduced me to your mother. She thought I was worthy enough to meet the sultana. Why don't you?"

"Does your friend know everything about you?" The words were dragged from his mouth. "Is she aware that you are the prince's mistress?"

"Of course not." Lacey said and rolled her eyes.

He speared a hard look at Lacey. She had spent half a year in his country but still didn't have a basic understanding how the Sultanate of Rudaynah worked. He risked everything to help her tonight. It would be scandalous if he were found alone with a woman. If it were discovered that she was his mistress, the results would be cataclysmic.

"I'm sorry if my meeting the sultana made you uncomfortable," she said angrily.

Was she? Had she not suggested a few days ago how he was better off without that title? Lacey had to be furious that her dream life ended abruptly while he was offered the one thing he had relentlessly worked toward. It wouldn't take much to crush his chances, but Hafiz didn't want to believe Lacey could be that diabolical.

"No, you're not. You want me to be uncomfortable and worry. You're enjoying it." Hafiz grabbed a hold of the door as the limousine took a sharp, fast turn. "I want to know the whole truth. How long have you known my mother?"

"I just met her," Lacey insisted. "It's not like we had an in-depth conversation."

Hafiz shook his head. Her eyes shone with innocence, and yet he didn't trust that the meeting was happenstance. She could have arranged to meet the sultana and dropped a few bombshells. He didn't want to think of how many times those blue eyes possibly duped him in the past.

"I swear, I didn't tell her anything."

And yet, despite careful planning of keeping his family and private life separate, his mother managed to meet his mistress. "This is not happening," he muttered. Being introduced to a mistress or concubine was considered a deep offense to the sultana. If the truth came out, he would pay the penalty for it. "You planned this, didn't you?"

"Planned what? An introduction with your mother?" Lacey asked listlessly, as if the fight had evaporated from her. She looked out the window at the dusty city streets whizzing past them.

"You hinted at it when you first arrived here. How you wanted to meet my family. Then it turned into a bold request and finally a demand."

Lacey rubbed her hands over her face and gave a deep sigh. "That was before I understood our relationship was completely forbidden. That I was somehow beneath you and not good enough to meet your family."

Beneath him? Where did she get that idea? "I told you that it was complicated."

"But you didn't tell me that it was impossible." She returned her attention to the window as if she couldn't bear to look at him. "I should have known something was up when you didn't introduce me to your friends. I was so naïve."

"I have nothing to apologize for."

She shook her head. "You brought me over here under false pretenses. I thought we were going to live together."

Hafiz's mouth dropped open in surprise. "I never made that offer. Us, together in the palace?" He shuddered at the thought. "We would have been cast out in seconds."

"Obviously you and I had different ideas

about being together. I didn't think you would hide my existence from your family."

"And when you realized that meeting them wasn't going to happen, you decided to take matters into your own hands."

"Like my introduction to your mother? What would be the point?" She turned to face him. "What do you think I did? Just walk up to her and say, 'Hi, I'm Lacey. I'm Hafiz's mistress and I hope to continue even after he's married?' Do you really think I'm capable of that?"

He stared at her with disbelieving horror as something close to panic clenched his stomach. "You would if you thought it would help."

"Help?" She watched him with growing suspicion. "Help what?"

"To stop me from getting married." She would eventually realize that he wasn't going to stop it. He accepted that his future wasn't going to be happy or loving. He had known that for the past decade.

"For the last time," she said, her voice rising, "I was not trying to wreck your wedding.

I am going against every instinct I have by not fighting for you." She tilted her head back and rested it against the seat. "Is that what makes you so suspicious? You gave me up and thought I would fight for you. For us. Because I immediately backed off, I must be up to something?"

"You think I gave you up easily? That there was no thought involved, no hesitation? I had put off my marriage for as long as possible so I could be with you."

"You put off your marriage so you could get a better deal," Lacey said through clenched teeth. "Like getting another shot at becoming the crown prince. Then you couldn't get rid of me fast enough."

"Lacey, I am not your parents. Try not to compare me with them. I didn't discard you to pursue my life's ambition."

Lacey's eyes narrowed into slits. "Don't bring my parents into this."

"You think I'm abandoning you out of ambition just like your parents. You act as if my life is going to overflow with happiness and abundance once you're out of my life. Do you think your parents had a better life without you?"

"Yes!" she bit out.

Hafiz drew his head back and stared at her. "You're wrong, Lacey. They missed out on so much."

"No, you are wrong. I held them back from what they really wanted in life. Once I was gone, they pursued their passion. They are happier than they've ever been."

Did she think he wouldn't look back at their time together? That he wouldn't feel the regret of letting her go? "Why do you act like I'm giving you up for something better? I am entering a marriage with a stranger," he reminded her.

"You made a choice, Hafiz. And it wasn't me. It was never going to be me."

A thought suddenly occurred to him. *She had been waiting for this to happen.* "You're not fighting for me because deep down you knew I was going to have to make a choice one day. And you knew it wasn't going to be in your favor."

"I'm not fighting for you because I know we have run our course." She gave a sharp intake of breath and tossed her hands in the air. "I should have just kept our relationship to a one-night stand and be done with you."

"Excuse me?" Anger flashed hot and swift inside him. What he and Lacey shared could not have been contained in one night.

"I knew you were trouble, but that didn't stop me. No, quite the opposite." She shook her head in self-disgust. "And, let's face it, you weren't thinking about forever after one night with me."

Hafiz wearily rubbed his hands over his eyes. "All I knew is that I couldn't stay away."

"And you kept coming back. I would count the days until we could see each other again. I thought you felt the same way, too."

"I did." The anticipation that burned in his veins, the excitement pressing against his chest had never waned.

"No, it's only been recently when I realized we had approached this affair very differently. I was so happy in love that I wanted to share it with the whole world. You wanted to keep this relationship secret because you were ashamed."

"For the last time, Lacey, I am not ashamed—"

"No, not of me." Her jaw trembled as she tried to hold her emotions in check. "You were ashamed that you couldn't stay away. After all those years of resisting temptation, of demonstrating your willpower, your strength, you couldn't stay away. An ordinary woman, a nobody, was your weakness."

He closed his eyes, momentarily overwhelmed. She was right. He didn't like how Lacey saw right through him. Understood him better than he understood himself.

"I am Prince Hafiz ibn Yusuf Qadi," he said quietly. "I have spent the last ten years proving that I am worthy of that name. I had purged every wild impulse, and nothing could tempt me off the straight and narrow path. And then I met you."

"You make me sound like I'm a vice. Something you need to give up to be a better person."

Hafiz was too deep into the memory to reply.

"And then I see you at the piano in a hotel lobby. I didn't even stop to think. I was drawn to your singing as if I was a sailor listening to the sirens."

"Being attracted to me does not show weakness of character. Falling for me is not a sin."

"It is if you are a prince from the Sultanate of Rudaynah."

She crossed her arms and stared at him. "And yet, you asked me to live here. I thought it was because you loved me. No, it's because you see me as some kind of bad habit that you couldn't give up."

Fury flashed through him, and he held it in check. "You don't have that kind of power over me. No one does."

"Especially a young woman who doesn't understand the royal court politics or influential people. That's why you felt safe to bring me over here."

He scoffed at her statement. "Having you here was never safe."

"I thought you trusted me. I thought that made

me different from everyone you knew. It made me special to you. But that's not it at all, is it? It's that you contained the situation. You made sure I wasn't in a position to break your trust."

"Not a lot of good it did me," he muttered.

Lacey's fingers fluttered against her cheeks as if she was brushing something away. "I wish I didn't know any of this. I wish I could have left Rudaynah the night I found out about your engagement."

Hafiz remained silent. He knew he should feel the same way. She was his weakness, his vulnerability, but he didn't want her to go.

"That night had been magical," she said softly. There was a faraway look in her eyes. "It was the right way to say goodbye. I would have left here believing that…what we had was special. That I had been special."

Hafiz clenched his hands. He wanted to tell Lacey how special she was to him. But what purpose would it serve? What they had was over. It could not continue.

"You think I'm bad for you," Lacey said. "That

I'm proof of your bad judgment, or that I symbolize all of those wild impulses you couldn't get rid of. One of these days you're going to realize that I was the best thing that had ever happened to you." She pointed her finger at him. "Someday you'll realize that everything I've done was to protect you."

"I don't need your protection, Lacey." He shook his head. "It was my job to protect you."

Lacey blinked rapidly as if she was preventing more tears from falling. "I wanted to be your confidante. Your partner. My goal was to help you be the best prince you could be."

"And in return, you would become a princess." Hafiz grimaced. Even as he said it, he knew that wasn't her true motivation.

"If you believe that, you don't know me at all." Her shoulders drooped as if she didn't have the energy to fight anymore. "I thought you knew everything about me," Lacey announced dully as she pulled her hair away from her face.

"And you know everything about me," Hafiz said. "I confided in you when I shouldn't have."

Lacey jerked at his harsh tone and slowly turned to meet his gaze. "Why do you continue to believe that I would betray you?"

Her question was carried out with a wispy puff of air. The wounded look in her eyes threatened to shatter him inside. He drew from the dark edges that hovered around him, knowing he had to be callous, and knowing he was going to regret it.

"Because you are a mistress. A fallen woman. Betrayal is your only power against me." Hafiz knew what he said hurt her where she was most vulnerable, but it was his only guarantee. That cold response would prevent Lacey from trying to hold on to him and what might have been. He had to protect her even if it meant tearing down the love she felt for him.

The darkness surged through Hafiz, and he struggled against the cold bitterness invading his body. He'd battled it before, only this time he had to do it alone. In the past, Lacey was the only person he knew who could stem the flow.

"If I'm a fallen women, you shouldn't be seen

with me. So, why are you still here?" Lacey asked in a withering tone. She folded her arms more tightly and crossed her legs. Hafiz wondered if it was an attempt to get as far away from him as possible. "Stop the car and I'll get out."

"That's enough." Hafiz's tone held a steely edge. "I'm making sure you get on that helicopter."

She gave a haughty tilt of her chin. "I'm perfectly capable of finding my way."

"I'm sure you could, but you don't have access to the palace."

"Palace?" Hafiz saw her tense as a sound of panic rumbled in the back of her throat; she turned abruptly to her window. When she didn't see anything on her side of the limousine, she frantically searched out his window.

He knew the minute she saw the towering mud brick walls that surrounded the palace. The historical site was constructed as more of a fortress than the home of a sultan. It wasn't opulent or majestic. The curved buildings, domed roofs and large archways were made out of clay. The buildings were functional and cool against the desert heat.

It was also designed to intimidate the enemy. Lacey had a look of unease as they passed through the guarded gates, and she got the first good look of the palace. Hafiz held back his assurances. He needed her to focus on leaving without looking back.

"I can't see you again," he began.

Her eyes dulled with pain. "I don't want you to."

Hafiz scowled at her statement. "I mean it, Lacey."

"I do, too. I'm not really big on sharing." Her chin wobbled, and she blinked back the moisture from her eyes. "Don't contact me unless you've changed your mind and only want me."

That wasn't going to happen, Hafiz thought. It couldn't.

The limousine lurched to a stop next to the helicopter pad. Hafiz immediately stepped out of the car and reached for Lacey's hand. When she hesitated, he grasped her wrist. Fierce sensations scorched his skin from the touch. He grimly ignored the way his pulse tripped and assisted her outside.

Her long hair blew in the desert wind, and he escorted her to the pilot who was waiting by the helicopter. After Hafiz yelled instructions over the noise, Lacey climbed in. He tried to assist her, but she batted him away. He flashed a warning look at her.

The warning dissipated as he looked into her eyes. Even after what had happened, after everything they'd said, he wished for one more kiss. He was desperate for it and felt the pull. His mouth craved her taste and her softness. The yearning pierced at him like swift jabs of a knife, because he knew after this moment, circumstances would snatch Lacey away from him.

He looked away. The darkness inside him eclipsed the pain of knowing this was the last time he would see her. Their paths would never cross, and he could never contact her again. He wouldn't know where she lived or if she was safe. She would disappear but linger in his mind as he worried and wondered.

"Your Highness," the pilot shouted, breaking through Hafiz's thoughts. "We need to leave now."

Hafiz hesitated. He couldn't make a clean break from Lacey, no matter how much he wanted to. How much he needed to, for both their sakes.

He glanced at her and met her gaze. No tears escaped her eyes. She didn't speak. Didn't move, but he knew she struggled for composure. He knew her poise was for his benefit. It was her way to prove that she would be fine.

She looked so beautiful and elegant. Regal. Hafiz thought his heart was going to blast through the wall of his chest. Lacey was more beautiful than when he first saw her. He was fortunate to have known and loved her, and she would never know. His throat closed shut as his strength seeped out of his bones.

He had to tell her. He had thought it would be

kinder not to say anything. Not to give her the answer because it would have given her hope. Something to fight for. But he could not let her go with the belief that she didn't matter.

"I love you, Lacey."

Her lips parted, and she stared at his mouth. She frowned as if she had heard incorrectly. As if she had heard what she wanted to hear.

"You may think I hate you or I'm ashamed of you," he said over the whine of the helicopter, "but it isn't true. I took all of these risks because I love you. I will always love you."

She began to reach out as the helicopter started to lift off. Hafiz wanted to grab her hand, but he forced himself to back away.

He watched her, unblinking, as the helicopter rose into the sky and turned, taking his love, his last chance of happiness, away from him.

But he didn't deserve happiness. He didn't deserve a life with Lacey.

Hafiz remained where he stood when every instinct screamed for him to run after Lacey. A ragged gasp escaped his raw throat as he watched the helicopter fly off until it was no longer a speck in the air. The silence sliced deep into his dreams and wishes until they lay tattered at his feet and darkness descended in his heart.

CHAPTER NINE

"LACEY, MY WORK shift is about to start," Priya shouted over the music. "Are you going to be okay? I feel weird leaving you alone."

"That's sweet of you, but you don't have to worry." Lacey smiled at her roommate. She felt bad that Priya felt the need to mother her. And drag her to this party so she would get out of the apartment. "I'm going to be fine. It's been a while since I've been to a party, but it's all coming back to me."

"Good," Priya said with a nod. "I know you've been mending a broken heart, but you are too young to spend all your time working at the hotel and staying in bed."

"You're right," she said as her roommate walked away. Taking a small sip from the beer bottle she had been nursing for an hour, Lacey

stood at the sidelines and watched her cowork-
ers mill around the pool room located in their
housing complex. It was an eclectic mix of
young people in swimwear and colorful sun-
dresses. While some splashed around in the
pool and others danced to the blaring music,
most of the guests nibbled on the spicy snacks
and drank the boldly colored concoctions.

Once Priya left the party, Lacey closed her
eyes and exhaled. She would stay another five
minutes and then leave.

She still wasn't sure why she'd chosen to stay
in Abu Dhabi, but it had proven to be a good
decision. The rich nightlife had allowed her to
find a job performing at the hotel lounge. She'd
also managed to make a few friends within the
month she arrived. She was determined to get
out and meet more people. Forget the past and
make up for lost time.

Sometimes determination wasn't enough. Her
time in Rudaynah had changed her. Marked her
in ways she hadn't considered. Lacey glanced
down at the purple bikini she wore and the

wispy sarong around her hips. These days she wasn't comfortable showing too much skin. She preferred the modest dress code she had to follow once she was outside the housing complex.

"Lacey!" Cody, another American who worked in the hotel, was at her side. His wide smile, unbuttoned shirt and bright red swim trunks conveyed his casual attitude toward life. He liked to flirt with her, and while she knew it didn't mean anything, she tried to discourage it.

"You haven't danced once the whole time you've been here." He held out his hand. "We need to fix that."

She hesitated for a second. She knew the invitation wasn't going to jump-start her love life, but the idea of dancing with another man— touching another man—felt wrong.

It's just a dance. It's no big deal. But she knew Cody would try for more. How could she explain to him that she didn't feel whole or intact? That she was definitely not strong enough to even expose herself to a lighthearted fling or a one-night stand?

Looking into Cody's face lined by the sun rather than by hardship, Lacey realized falling in love again was impossible. She felt the corners of her mouth quirk as she considered her foolishness. What was she worried about? She was safe with Cody and every other man. No one could measure up to Hafiz.

"Okay, sure. Why not?" She set down her beer and took his hand. Lacey didn't feel any thrill of anticipation when he placed his other hand on the curve of her hip or when her fingers grazed his bare skin. She felt no excitement, no awareness. Nothing.

But, quite honestly, she hadn't felt a thing since the helicopter touched down in Abu Dhabi a month ago. She went through the motions of living, but she felt dead inside. She had a feeling it was going to be like that forever. And still she didn't worry over the possibility.

As Lacey danced in Cody's arms, she wondered how long the song would last. She knew that if Hafiz had been her dance partner, she would have wanted the music to go on forever.

Hafiz. She had to stop thinking about him. Lacey abruptly pulled away just as the song changed into something harsh and angry.

Cody motioned for her to keep dancing, but she wanted to go home. No, that wasn't true. She wanted to find Hafiz.

But that was not going to happen, Lacey reminded herself. He didn't want her near him. She was a vice. A sin. Hafiz's words ricocheted through her head. Nothing had changed. Nothing ever would. She had to move on.

"Don't hold back, Lacey!" Cody yelled as he jumped up and down to the drumbeat.

Move on. Start now. Fake it until you make it. Lacey swayed to the music. She wished it had the power to make her forget everything. But the music didn't reach her heart or fill her soul like it used to.

She needed to feel it again. Music was part of who she was. It was more than her livelihood; it was how she expressed herself and how she found solace. She couldn't let Hafiz take that away from her, too.

Lacey pushed harder as she danced. She moved her shoulders and swished her hips to the beat of the drums. The music still didn't reach her.

She pulled and pushed her body to move as far as it would go, wishing that the numbness that held everything back would break. That the music would grow louder until it seeped inside her. If that didn't work, then she hoped the dancing would exhaust her so she could sleep without dreaming.

From the corner of her eyes, Lacey saw that someone wore all black. A jacket...no, a suit. The formality was at odds with the party. The darkness was out of place among the bright rainbow colors. But there was something familiar about the person's movement. What was it that... Her heart lurched, and she went still.

Hafiz. She froze as the wild hope and surprise ripped through her. Hafiz was here? No, that was impossible. She blinked, and he was suddenly gone. Lacey rubbed her eyes. Was she now having hallucinations about him along with her dreams?

Her pulse skipped hard as she quickly scanned the crowd. Why did he seem so real? Shouldn't her memory become hazier as time went on?

She frowned as she resumed her dancing. Her memory was definitely playing tricks. Lacey didn't understand why she envisioned him in a black linen jacket, collarless shirt and black trousers. Usually she remembered him in a pinstripe suit, in traditional robes, or in nothing at all.

Lacey squeezed her eyes shut as she tried to discard the images of Hafiz in various stages of undress flickering through her mind. *Forget about him,* she decided as she forced herself to dance. *It's time to start living again.*

Hafiz watched Lacey dance, her body moving with the same earthiness as when they shared a bed. It had been four weeks since he'd seen Lacey. Since he had declared his love. It felt like an eternity. He shouldn't be here, and yet he couldn't stay away.

Now he wished he hadn't given in to the impulse. Anger and indignation swirled inside him, ready to explode. From what he could see, Lacey was the center of the party. She wasn't laughing or smiling, but her intense expression suggested that nothing mattered more than exploring the music.

He glared at the bikini and sarong she wore. It flaunted her curves instead of hiding them. The bikini top lovingly clung to her breasts. Her nipples pressed against the fragile fabric. The sarong hung low, emphasizing her tiny waist and the gentle swell of her hips.

His gaze traveled down her taut stomach. The ivory skin was sun-kissed, but she had lost weight. Pining for him? Hafiz glanced around the party and scoffed at the idea as he crossed his arms. He wished. More like too much partying.

The brightly colored sarong teased his senses, and he couldn't drag his gaze away from her bare legs. He remembered how they felt wrapped around his waist as he drove into her.

When Lacey rolled her hips, Hafiz's restraint threatened to shatter. Where was a voluminous caftan when you needed one? He was beginning to see the advantages.

Lacey was surrounded by cheering men, and she unknowingly taunted them with the thrust of her hips. Hafiz swore she was more sensual than any belly dancer without even trying. Did she know that these men would do anything to get her into bed? They couldn't hide the desperation to take his place in her life.

Had they already?

The possibility fueled his bitter jealousy. He could not hold back any longer. He stepped through the circle of the men posturing for Lacey's attention and reached for her. Hafiz grasped her wrist and was painfully aware of the heat coursing through him from the simple touch.

Lacey opened her eyes just as he slid her against him. Blood sang through his veins as her soft breasts pressed against his hard chest. He shuddered as his control slipped. After a month without her, every primal instinct told him to pounce and never let her go.

"Miss me, Lacey?" he murmured in her ear.

He watched as she blinked at him. His chest ached as he waited, wondering how she would greet him. Would she push him away? Would she welcome him with the same cool friendliness she'd welcome an old acquaintance? Or would she treat him with indifference?

"Hafiz?"

He drew her closer as the people and the noise faded around them. He had eyes only for Lacey. She pressed her hands to his face. "I can't believe you're here," she whispered.

He held her hand and pressed his mouth against her palm. "You did miss me," he said, purring with satisfaction.

"Of course I did." She wrapped her arms around his neck and held him fiercely. "How can you ask?" she asked against his chest.

"Let's get out of here," he insisted as he drew

her away. He was too impatient to taste Lacey's mouth on his. He needed her more than his next breath. "I want you all to myself."

Hafiz held her hand tightly as he guided her out of the party as if he couldn't risk losing her. As if she might break away. He was striding to the elevators that would whisk them to her apartment when he abruptly turned and pulled her into a shadowy corner.

It had been too long. He wasn't going to wait anymore. He pressed her back against the corner and braced his arms against the walls, trapping her. "Show me how much you missed me."

Lacey didn't hesitate and claimed Hafiz's mouth with hers. The one touch, one kiss, was all it took for the numbness to disappear. Her skin tingled, her heart pounded against her chest, and blood roared in her ears as she violently came back to life.

She still couldn't believe it. Hafiz had come for her. He chose her over his fiancée and his duty. Over his country. He chose *her*.

Lacey pulled away and stared at Hafiz. She searched his face, noticing how much he had changed in a month. His features were harsher, the lines and angles more pronounced. The sexual hunger in his eyes was ferocious.

She trembled with anticipation and grabbed his jacket lapels. Hafiz wrapped his hands around her waist and ripped off her sarong. He tossed it on the ground with an impatience she'd never seen in him.

She knew Hafiz was almost out of his mind with lust. He was desperate to touch her. To taste her. She understood this driving need, but the intensity was almost painful. She felt as if she could explode from it.

Hafiz pushed the bikini top away and exposed her breasts. They felt heavy under his hot gaze. Lacey almost wept as Hafiz captured one tight nipple in his mouth. She raked her fingers through his hair, encouraging him closer.

Lacey gasped at the primal, almost savage way he stripped her bikini bottoms from her hips. She could tell that his control was slipping. He couldn't hold back. This reunion was going to be hard, fast and furious.

She couldn't believe she had this power over him. That they had this power over each other. Lacey liked how his fingers shook as he tore the flimsy piece of fabric from her trembling legs. She bit her lip when he roughly cupped her sex.

"Now," she muttered. "I need you in me now."

Hafiz didn't follow her demands. Instead he dipped his fingers into her wet heat. Lacey panted hard as her flesh gripped him tight and drew him in deeper.

As Hafiz stroked her with his fingers, Lacey pressed her mouth shut to prevent a throaty moan from escaping. They were hidden as the party continued around them. No one could hear them, no one could see, but old habits died hard. She couldn't risk being discovered, but she couldn't bear the idea of stopping.

Lacey dove her hands under his shirt and slid her fingers along his hot, flushed skin. She wanted to rip his clothes off his perfect body, but that would take too much time. She smiled when his breath hitched in his throat as his muscles bunched under her touch. He countered with the flick of his finger inside her. She shuddered as the fiery sensations swept through her body.

"Now, Hafiz. I can't wait any longer." She heard the metallic sound of his zipper and rocked her hips with impatience. She gulped for air and inhaled the musky scent of his arousal. Her chest ached with excitement as he lifted her up and hooked her legs over his hips.

He entered her with one smooth thrust. Hafiz's long groan rumbled from his chest, and he didn't move as if he was savoring this moment. His penis stretched and filled her, but Lacey couldn't stay still. She wanted more—needed everything Hafiz had to give her. She rolled her pelvis slowly and was rewarded with a warning growl before he clenched his fingers into her hips. Hafiz withdrew and plunged into her again and again.

She eagerly accepted each wild thrust. Lacey held on to Hafiz tightly and closed her eyes as her climax forked through her. Her heart faltered as the fury rushed through, taking the last of her strength. Her mind grasped on the only thing that mattered—he had chosen her above all else.

"This bed is too small," Hafiz complained in a murmur as he held Lacey in his arms. She lay on top of him, naked and warm. She rested her head against his chest, and he threaded his fingers through her long hair.

He was right where he wanted to be.

"It's fine," she said sleepily.

Fine? He shook his head at the thought. His feet dangled off the edge, and his shoulders were almost too wide for the bed. The mattress was as thin and cheap as the sheets.

It was too dark to see all of Lacey's bedroom, but he could tell that it was tiny with just a few furnishings. It was nothing like the apartment she had in Rudaynah.

"We should go to my hotel suite," Hafiz suggested. "It's more comfortable. Bigger." *Bet-*

ter. He felt Lacey deserved more. How did she wind up here?

"Mmm-hmm." Lacey made no move to get up.

He slid his hand down and caressed her spine. He felt her shiver of pleasure under his palm. "Do you like Abu Dhabi?" he asked.

"Mmm-hmm."

"Why did you choose to live here?" He had been astounded when he discovered she was still in the UAE. He thought she had gone home. Back to St. Louis. "Did you know someone? Had business contacts?"

"I didn't know anyone," she said with a yawn. "But I applied for some jobs, did the necessary paperwork, and I got this one at the hotel."

"Adventurous of you," Hafiz said as he cupped the base of her head and held her close. He didn't like the idea that she was all alone in the world. That there was no one looking out for her. Protecting her.

"You sound surprised," Lacey said. "May I remind you, I moved to Rudaynah sight unseen? Some people consider that adventurous. My friends thought it was crazy."

"That was different. You had me to take care of you."

"I've been looking after myself for as long as I can remember."

"You let me take care of you," Hafiz said. The words echoed in his mind. She *let* him. She had given her trust in so many ways, and he took it for granted.

"It wasn't easy for me," Lacey admitted as she pressed her mouth against his chest and gave him a kiss. "I didn't want to be dependent on you."

Lacey Maxwell wasn't cut out to be a mistress, Hafiz decided. Most women took the role because they wanted to be taken care of.

"What's wrong with depending on me?" he asked. "On anyone?"

"I remember what it was like when I had to rely on my parents. They really didn't want to deal with me."

His fingers tightened against her. Anger flared

inside him as he imagined a young Lacey, ignored and neglected. "You don't know that."

"I do." There was no sadness in her voice. She spoke as if she was giving the facts. "They have not reached out to me once I've been on my own. It's better this way. I know I made the right decision to cut them out of my life."

A cold chill swept through Hafiz. *"You're* the one that walked away?"

"I tried for years to be the daughter they wanted and needed. But I couldn't earn their love or attention. I walked away and didn't look back."

His heart started to race. He had always thought Lacey was tenacious. It was one of her most admirable traits. He had seen her practice a piece of music until she got it right or talk him through a work problem even if it took all night. But even she had limits. "But…they're your parents."

"And that's why it took me so long to walk away. I kept thinking circumstances would change. But they didn't see any need to change.

They weren't being malicious. They were extremely selfish. It took me years to forgive them, but I'm not trying to make them love me anymore."

Hafiz couldn't shake the fear that gripped his chest. He had always felt that Lacey's love was unconditional. It was the one thing he could count on. Yet Lacey had walked away from the strongest bond a person could have. He thought that once Lacey loved someone, it was forever.

This changed everything.

"Lacey." She felt a large hand cupping her shoulder, rousing her out of the best sleep she'd had in a long, long time. "Lacey, wake up."

She peered through bleary eyes. A whisper of a smile formed on her lips when she saw Hafiz looking down at her. Last night hadn't been a dream. "Come back to bed," she mumbled drowsily and patted the mattress next to her.

"It's time to get up, Sleeping Beauty," he said with a smile.

She looked at him and noticed for the first

time that he was already dressed in his black T-shirt and trousers. His hair gleamed with dampness from a recent shower.

Lacey sighed and stretched, murmuring in protest at the twinges in her muscles. "Sleeping Beauty isn't my favorite fairytale princess," she said as she rubbed the sleep from her eyes.

"You prefer Rapunzel?" he asked. "I finally read that fairy tale you kept talking about."

"Really?" She slowly sat up in bed and pushed her hair away from her face. "What did you think of it?"

Hafiz's mouth set in a grim line. She suspected he was going to ask something but wasn't sure if he would like the answer. "Did you see me as the prince who saved the day, or did you see me as the witch who trapped Rapunzel in the tower?"

Lacey blinked, startled by the question. The corners of her lips tilted into a sad smile as she wrapped the bed sheet around her nude body. "It took me a while before I realized that you were the Rapunzel in the story."

Hafiz jerked his head back. "That's not funny."

"I'm serious. Think about it," she said. She knew she should have kept her opinion to herself. What man would want to be compared to Rapunzel? But it was too late, and she needed to explain her way of thinking. "Rudaynah was your tower and you were trapped."

"I am not trapped," he said stiffly. "I have duties and obligations, but that is not the same thing."

"Those expectations were holding you back. The sultan was more interested in how you acted than what you accomplished."

"I don't want to talk about that right now." The flash of annoyance in Hafiz's eyes indicated that the topic would be discussed at length later.

"It doesn't matter. It's the past. You're free now," she said with a wide smile. "You escaped the tower. Although I'm sure you would want to visit the sultanate every once in a while. It is your homeland."

Hafiz tilted his head and stared at her with incomprehension. "Lacey, what are you talking about?"

"You left Rudaynah. Didn't you?" she asked slowly. "We agreed that we wouldn't see each other unless you chose me and only me."

"I never agreed to that."

She tried to remember what had been said that night. Hafiz had said he loved her. It was the one thing that held her together when she wondered what it all had been for.

"You love me. You found me," she said softly. "But you're not staying?"

Hafiz sighed. "No."

She flinched as his answer clawed at her. It tore her to shreds before she had a chance to ward off the pain. "And you're still..."

"Getting married. Yes."

Those three words ripped away the last fragment of hope. She closed her eyes and hunched her shoulders. Hafiz hadn't chosen her. He hadn't chased her across the world to get her back.

CHAPTER TEN

HE WAS STILL getting married to Nabeela. The stark truth sliced through her. He'd failed to mention that important piece of information before he possessed her body and soul throughout the night. The rat. The snake.

She couldn't believe he would do this to her. Again. How many times would she fall for this routine? "Get out," she ordered hoarsely, clutching the sheet against her.

"What?" Arrogant disbelief tinged his voice.

"I thought you chose me. I'm such a fool," she whispered, gently rocking back and forth. It felt as if she was bleeding inside. She was going to drown in it.

Hafiz exhaled sharply. "I am choosing to be with you."

"Temporarily," she said. "You came here for

sex." She stiffened and looked at the bed before scrambling off of the mattress. She gave a fierce yank to the bed sheets that covered her body. Her body, which she'd freely given to him with her love hours before.

He splayed his hands in the air. "I didn't plan it."

"Right." This from a man who was in control of everything and everyone around him. "You didn't plan to travel to Abu Dhabi. You didn't plan to search for me. You didn't plan to take me against a wall minutes after you found me."

He rolled his shoulders back as if he was bracing himself for a direct hit. "I traveled here for a meeting. I'm staying at this hotel, and I didn't know you were still in Abu Dhabi until I saw the poster at the hotel lounge about your performance."

Just when she thought she couldn't feel any worse. He hadn't come here just to find her. He didn't go out of his way to seek her. She stared at Hafiz, not sure if she was going to burst into

tears or start laughing maniacally at the unfairness of it all.

She needed to cover herself. Protect herself.
Lacey grabbed her robe that had fallen on the
floor. "You needed to scratch an itch. Why?
Your fiancée won't sleep with you until the
wedding night?"

His eyes darkened. "I have no contact with
my future bride because it is an arranged marriage. It is not a love match."

As if that was supposed to make her feel better. The muscle in her cheek twitched with fury.
"It's probably best that way. You don't want her
to find out how rotten to the core you are until
after the vows are exchanged."

"Lacey, I apologize for the misunderstanding."

"Misunderstanding? There was no misunderstanding. You withheld that information
because if I knew you were still engaged, I
wouldn't have welcomed you with open arms."

"Don't be too sure. We have a connection that
is too—"

"Connection?" She gave a harsh laugh. "No, we have a past. That is it. You severed that connection when you got me out of your life as quickly as possible."

"We still have something," he argued. "That's why I came to check up on you and—"

"You came to have sex because you're not used to going without." Lacey thrust her arms through the sleeves of her robe. The fiery orange silk felt like needles across her sensitive skin. "And you knew I wouldn't deny you. Especially since you had lied to me and said you loved me."

Hafiz drew back. "That wasn't a lie."

She glared at him, fighting the urge to strike out with her nails unsheathed. "Your timing was suspicious."

He placed his hands on his hips. "Suspicious?"

"You tell me that you love me the moment before I was out of your life forever. Was it a way to keep me dangling on your hook? That way, when you looked me up, you didn't have to work too hard to get back into my bed."

"I told you in a moment of weakness," he said in a low growl. "I didn't want you to look back and think the year we spent together meant nothing."

Their time had meant everything to her. It had been the one time when she felt safe and wanted. She had honestly believed during the months in Rudaynah that they had been growing closer and that their relationship could weather anything.

"You could have told me you loved me at any time, but you didn't. Why?" She took a step closer and pointed her finger accusingly at him. "Because saying those words at the last minute meant you didn't have to do anything about it."

He raked his fingers through his hair. Lacey had the feeling he wanted to grab her by the shoulders and shake her. She took a prudent step back.

"If you don't believe me," Hafiz said in a clipped tone, "that is your problem."

Lacey glared at him. Wouldn't a man in love want to express his emotions? Wouldn't he show it with grand gestures and small, intimate moments?

But not this man. No, not Prince Hafiz. He wasn't going to lower himself and try to convince her. He wasn't going to waste his energy on proving something that didn't exist.

"You want to forget everything I did for you? For us? Go right ahead," Hafiz said. "I love you and nothing is going to change that."

"What am I supposed to think? You say you love me when you are engaged to another woman." She tied the sash of her robe with enough force that it could have ripped.

Hafiz ground the heels of his palms against his eyes. "I'm not replacing you."

"Of course not," Lacey said as she walked out of the bedroom. "I would have had to be part of your life for Nabeela to replace my role."

Hafiz followed her into the main room with long, brisk strides. His presence made the apartment feel smaller, as if it couldn't contain him. Lacey wished Priya had not had the night shift. She wanted him to leave and could have used some backup right now. Knowing what kind of man he was, Hafiz wouldn't leave until he got what he was after.

"You made sure I wasn't part of your world," Lacey continued. "I thought I needed to earn that privilege because I was a foreigner and a nobody. Now I realize that nothing I did would have made a difference. It just wasn't going to happen."

She was done trying to earn love. It didn't work. She had twisted and bent herself into knots, determined to give her all and make her relationships work. She had made Hafiz the most important part of her life, and he could not do the same. He had accepted her love as if it was his due, but he did not see her as a priority in life.

No more. Hafiz did not value her role in his life, and he wasn't going to. From now on, she would put herself first because no one else would. She would not settle or compromise.

She heard Hafiz's cell phone ring. Lacey

whirled around and saw him retrieve it from his pocket. "Don't you dare."

He frowned as he glanced up from the touch screen. "I'm just—"

"No, you are not answering that phone. I don't care if Rudaynah suddenly disappeared from the face of the earth. It can't be as important as what's going on here."

"Lacey, don't be—"

"I'm serious, Hafiz. For once, I am your top priority. The most important person in your life is right in front of you, so put the phone away."

Hafiz's austere face tightened, clearly holding his anger in check.

"If you'd rather take the call," she said coldly, "then leave and don't come back."

Her heart was pounding as the phone continued to ring. Hafiz silently turned off the ringer and returned the phone to his pocket as he held her gaze.

Lacey tried to hide her surprise. She had never given him an ultimatum like that. She had always been reluctant, always knowing that he held the power in the relationship. She'd believed that if she made any demands, placed any expectations on him, he would exchange her for another woman.

It turned out that he'd done it anyway.

"I am marrying Nabeela, but the marriage is in name only," Hafiz assured her.

"What exactly does that mean?"

"It means that we will not live in the same suite of rooms in the palace. It means that we will see each other on official occasions, and, even then, we won't stand next to each other."

Lacey's eyes narrowed as she listened to his explanation. "And this is what you want?"

"It's not about what I want to do. It's about meeting my obligations. Meeting the expectations of my country and my family."

"Will you consummate the marriage?"

His nostrils flared as he reined in his patience. "It is required by law."

The idea of him in bed with another woman made her sick to her stomach. How would he feel if she chose to sleep with another man?

Claimed it was required? Hafiz would do everything in his power to prevent that from happening. Why did he think she wouldn't respond in the same way? Because she was a woman? Because as a mistress she had no claim on him?

"Will you have children?" she asked.

The muscle in his jaw twitched. "As the second in line to the throne, I am not required to have an heir."

She noticed he didn't answer her question. "But you won't be second in line," she reminded him. "You will be the crown prince if you marry Nabeela."

"That is the sultan's promise, but I don't know if or when it will happen. I need to be the crown prince," Hafiz admitted. "I didn't expect to get a second chance, and I have to take it."

"It's what you want most," she said in a matter-of-fact tone. He wanted it more than he wanted her. "It's what you strove for all these years."

"I had abused that power ten years ago. If

I get the title back, I can make amends. I can show that I'm different. That I am the leader that they need."

Power. It was all about the power. "But the sultan has the ultimate power. And he can strip your title whenever he sees fit."

"That is true, but I won't let that happen. I know how to protect what is mine. This time no one will intimidate or harm those who are important to me. This time I have the power to fight back."

Lacey shook her head with resignation. That sounded like the Hafiz she knew and loved. "You already have that power," she pointed out. "You don't need to be a prince to use it."

He reared his head back as if she had said something blasphemous. "I disagree. Taking care of Rudaynah is my purpose in life. I can't do that if I'm not their prince."

Lacey tried to imagine what Hafiz would be like without a royal title. He would still be arrogant and influential. People would continue to clamor for his attention and advice. But would his countrymen allow him to represent the sultanate if he wasn't a prince, or would they treat him as a celebrity? She didn't know.

"I may not agree with you every time, Lacey, but I always listened. You made me look at the world differently. I missed the way we used to talk," Hafiz said.

Lacey looked away. "We didn't talk. I was your mistress, not your girlfriend. We had sex. Lots and lots of sex."

"Don't," Hafiz said harshly. "Stop rewriting our history."

Was she guilty of that? Lacey sank her teeth into her bottom lip. She had felt loved and adored when she was with Hafiz. He had been generous and caring. Maybe it wasn't just about sex.

"Think about the times you listened to the troubles I had on a project or my concerns for the sultanate," Hafiz said quietly. "You gave me advice and ideas. I knew I could count on you to give me honest feedback. Your opinion always mattered to me."

"And now you have Nabeela for that."

"Nabeela won't look after my best interest. She can't drive me wild. She can't love me the way you do."

"Then break the engagement," she whispered.

He froze and turned his head away. "No, Lacey," Hafiz said as he took a step back.

"You don't have to do this to redeem yourself. You have made up for your mistakes years ago."

"I don't deserve forgiveness."

"You don't deserve a loveless marriage," she insisted. "I know what it's like to be unloved. To be surrounded by indifference. It chips away at you until you become a shadow of yourself."

"I can't break the engagement. It's too late."

Lacey closed her eyes as the pain flashed through her. "And you can't walk away from me. So, what do you plan to do?" She slowly opened her eyes as it occurred to her. "You plan to have both of us?" she asked in a scandalized whisper.

Hafiz remained silent as he watched her closely.

She felt the blood drain from her face. "You need to leave right now. I can't believe you would insult me this way."

"I told you, my marriage would be in name only. It's not a real marriage. It's not even a relationship."

She thrust her finger at the door. "Get out," she said, her voice trembling with outrage.

Hafiz sighed and went to collect his jacket. "Give me one good reason why this won't work."

"I don't want to be your mistress." At one time in her life, she gladly accepted the role. It had been the only way she could be in his life. She'd gratefully accepted the crumbs he offered, but now she knew she deserved more.

"But you can't be my wife," he murmured.

"You made sure that couldn't happen. Even if you didn't accept Nabeela as your bride, I still wouldn't be your wife. Because I was a mistress. *Your* mistress."

"That's not the only reason."

"Because you don't think I'm worthy of the title."

"That's not true," he said, grabbing her wrists with his large hands, forcing her to stand still as he towered over her. "I love you and I want to spend the rest of my life with you. This is the best compromise I can make."

"Compromise." Her lips curled with disgust as she said the word. "I'm done compromising."

"There are rules," he said in an impatient growl.

"Break them," she suggested wildly. "You've done it before."

"And I regret it every day. This is different."

"Here's a thought. Stop hiding me from the world and present me to your family with pride. Show them that it's not a sin to love me. Tell them that I am everything you need and that I'm the one you will marry."

"That isn't going to happen. Ever."

Lacey looked down at her bare feet. She had gone too far. She had made an ultimatum that showed the limit of his love for her. She should have known, should have been happy with what he offered, but she couldn't. She wasn't going to take a smaller and demeaning role just to stay in his life. That wasn't love. That was the first step on the path to her destruction.

She had to protect herself. She suddenly felt weak, so much so she couldn't raise her head to meet his gaze. Lacey took a deep breath, the air hurting her raw throat and tight chest.

"And this, what we had together, isn't going to happen again," she said in a low rush. It took all of her strength to raise her head and meet his gaze. "I need you to leave now."

She saw the calculating gleam in his eye just as she heard a key fumbling in the lock of the front door. Lacey turned just as her roommate rushed in.

"Lacey! Why haven't you been answering your texts?" Priya asked as she slammed the door closed.

Priya looked flustered. Her topknot threatened to collapse, and her name tag was crookedly pinned on her black blazer. She appeared out of breath, and her face gleamed with sweat.

"Are you all right?" Lacey asked as her roommate openly studied Hafiz. "Priya, this is—"

Priya raised her hand. "Prince Hafiz, the guy who broke her heart."

Lacey straightened her spine and clutched the lapels of her robe. "How do you know that? I never told you his name."

"No need." Priya swiped her finger against the screen of her phone. "It's all right here in full color."

"What are you talking about?" The lethal tone in Hafiz's low voice made Priya hesitate.

"This." She turned the phone around to show a picture of Hafiz and Lacey in a hot embrace at the party. It was a good quality picture from someone's phone. There was no denying that Prince Hafiz was the man in the picture. Lacey's face was partially hidden, but her identity didn't matter. The fact that her bikini-clad body was plastered against Hafiz was damning enough.

The sharp twist of dread in Lacey's stomach almost made her sick. She clapped a shaky hand against her mouth.

"How many pictures are there?" Hafiz asked.

Lacey's gaze clashed with his. Her eyes widened as she remembered those stolen moments in the corridor outside the party. They hadn't been aware of their surroundings as they made love. What if their recklessness had been caught on camera?

Oh, God. What had they done? It had been madness. Lacey watched Hafiz's gaze harden, no doubt considering the repercussions.

"I've only seen this one so far."

So far. Lacey wanted to sit down before she tumbled to the floor. Hafiz was right. She was his vice. No, she was his poison. She was going to ruin everything for him.

"Who sent it to you?" Lacey asked. "Maybe we can get them to delete it from their camera." Maybe they would luck out. Maybe one of their friends had no idea who Hafiz was and sent it to Priya because she was in the picture.

"I don't know," Priya said as she pressed the screen. "One of our friends was sharing pictures of the party. But it's only a matter of time before someone finds out Hafiz is the playboy prince. Once that happens, there's no containing this."

CHAPTER ELEVEN

HAFIZ STARED AT the image on the small screen. The picture revealed everything. He had greeted Lacey with an intensity that indicated they were more than acquaintances. The passion, the love, the desperate yearning was evident in his expression.

Why? Why hadn't he been more careful? He knew the risks. Did he think the rules only applied when he was home?

He hadn't been thinking. The moment he had seen Lacey's picture in the hotel lounge he had been on the hunt for her. He should have resisted the urge. He had not contacted Lacey for a month and managed to get through each day. But that didn't mean he hadn't thought of her constantly.

"Hafiz?"

He jerked at the sound of Lacey's voice. His gaze slammed into hers. He saw the concern and the tears. But it was the defeat in her eyes that slayed him. Lacey always looked at him as if he was invincible. That he could achieve the impossible.

Now she wasn't so sure. Not when it looked as if he would lose everything over a damning photo.

Priya cleared her throat and only then did Hafiz remember she was in the room. He was always like this when he was around Lacey. Nothing else mattered. It was becoming a major problem.

"I'm going to give you guys some privacy," the roommate said as she started to back away. "Lacey, text me when the prince is ready to return to his hotel suite."

"Why?" Lacey asked.

"If this picture gets out, other photographers will try to find me. A picture of me is worth a lot of money, especially if it includes you," Hafiz explained.

He remembered how this worked. It was humbling that he was in the same predicament that he'd found himself in ten years ago. It didn't matter how much he had tried to control his wilder impulses, he had not changed at all.

Priya nodded. "I can get you to your room unseen."

"Thank you." He returned his attention to Lacey. She crossed her arms tightly against her body and began to pace.

The moment Priya closed the door, Lacey whirled around to face him. "I had nothing to do with this."

Hafiz narrowed his eyes. He wasn't sure what Lacey was talking about, but he often found being silent was the best way to get information.

"I did not set you up," Lacey said. "I know you think that I'm out to sabotage your wedding, but I wouldn't do that."

"You wouldn't?" he asked softly. The thought hadn't crossed his mind. He knew his appearance had been unexpected, and Lacey's attention had been focused on him from the moment they had reconnected. He knew he could trust Lacey about this.

The fact that she immediately leaped to the conclusion that he would suspect her bothered him. He didn't trust easily, and yet he trusted Lacey more than anyone. But since his trust wasn't blind or absolute, Lacey thought he didn't trust her at all.

"Of course, I wouldn't. Do you think all mistresses are manipulative schemers who would do anything to maintain their lifestyles?"

"You aren't like any other mistress." Lacey hadn't been motivated by money, status or power.

"I wouldn't know. I have nothing to compare," Lacey said as she continued to pace. "But, believe me, I am not interested in returning to Rudaynah and maintaining the lifestyle of secrets and hiding."

"Hate Rudaynah that much?"

"I don't *hate* it," she corrected him. "There were parts of it that I found intolerable, but I also saw the beauty and wonder."

Hafiz doubted she could list what she found beautiful. "No, you hated it."

"I hated that I was separated from you," she said. "I hated that we had to hide our relationship."

"Our relationship is about to be brought out into the open," he murmured. He would have to deny it, but no one would believe him. It was clear in the photo that he was intimate with Lacey. And if they had photos of what happened immediately after that embrace... He would protect Lacey from the embarrassment, no matter the cost or the consequences.

"Do you think I forced your hand?" Lacey stopped pacing and stood directly in front of him. "I didn't. I don't know how to convince you that I have nothing to do with this picture. I don't have any proof. But once I find the person who is responsible..."

Hafiz was momentarily fascinated as he watched her shake her fist in the air. He hadn't seen her like this. She was in full protective mode. Of *him*. He took care of Lacey, not the other way around.

"I know you don't have anything to do with it," Hafiz said.

She lowered her fist and gave him a sidelong glance. "You do?" She said the words in a slow drawl.

Hafiz nodded. "It's not your nature." He knew that, but it hadn't stopped him from accusing her in the past. He had let his past experiences with women cloud his judgment.

"Just like that?" She snapped her fingers. "A month ago I couldn't have lunch with a few friends without you accusing me of betrayal."

"I had jumped to conclusions," he admitted. "I thought…"

"That I would retaliate because I was kicked out of your life with little ceremony?"

He felt his mouth twitch with displeasure at her description. Their relationship ended abruptly, but he did not kick her out.

"Something like that," he admitted. "I'm sorry I considered that was a possibility. I know you're not that kind of person. You are loyal and sweet. Innocent about the world, really."

"That's an unusual choice of words for a mistress."

He raked his fingers through his hair and exhaled. "Stop calling yourself a mistress."

She looked at him with surprise. "Why? That was my role in your life. We weren't a couple. We weren't partners. We led separate lives during the day and spent the nights together. Only you didn't stay all night."

"No, I didn't." It had been a test of willpower every night to get out of Lacey's bed and return to the palace.

"Where is this coming from?" Lacey asked as she planted her hands on her hips. "You don't have to pretty up the past, Hafiz."

"I don't want people to think the worst about you." He should have considered that before he brought her over to Rudaynah, but all he had cared about was having her near.

"You don't want them to know that I was a

mistress?" She tilted her head as she studied his expression. "Or is it that you don't want people to know about your role?"

Those words were like a punch in the stomach. Was that the real reason he didn't want Lacey to wear that label? He was a prince, was held to a higher standard, but he had brought Lacey to his world by any means necessary.

"Because deep down that goes against what you believe in, doesn't it, Hafiz? You don't want to be the playboy prince, but you had a kept woman. Instead of making a commitment or having a relationship based on mutual feelings, you made arrangements with a woman so you could have exclusive access to her body."

"Our relationship was more than just sex," Hafiz said in a growl. Not that anyone would see it that way.

"The palace may have some questions about that if they see that picture." Lacey dragged her hands down her face. "What are we going to do about it?"

Hafiz went still. "*We?* No, you aren't getting involved with this."

Lacey rolled her eyes. "We're in this together, and we're going to get out of it together."

He was conflicted. Hafiz had always appreciated it when Lacey was ready to fight alongside him, but he didn't want to drag her into this battle.

"No one can see your face in the picture," Hafiz insisted. "You can't be identified. Let's keep it that way."

"It's only a matter of time," Lacey said. "Someone at the party is going to remember what I wore and how you dragged me out of the party."

"It was late, and people had been drinking. No one can be too sure what happened."

"Anyway," she continued, "I don't care if people know it's me."

Why didn't Lacey care about her reputation? A public scandal never died. He hadn't thought much about his until he destroyed his reputation and took the slow, hard road to repair it. He knew it would be much worse for a woman.

"I care." Hafiz knew his voice sounded harsh, but he had to get Lacey to understand. "If you get caught up in a scandal with me, it will cling to you for the rest of your life. You will always be known as the woman who slept with the playboy prince."

Lacey lifted her chin. "I've done nothing to be ashamed about."

"Nothing?" he asked with a tinge of incredulity. "We lost control. We made compromises and excuses even when it went against everything we've been taught. Everything we believe in." He turned away from Lacey. "And even though we swear that we won't meet again, that we won't think about what might have been, we break our promises. The moment we see each other, we destroy everything we tried to create."

The silence pulsed between them.

She made him dream about a life he had no right to pursue. Hafiz winced as resentment shot through his chest. He took in a deep sigh, and he realized nothing had changed. No, that wasn't true. When he was with Lacey, everything he felt was sharper and stronger. Life after Lacey was going to be excruciating.

He needed to be strong and not give in to his wants. He had done that for years until he met Lacey. After disappointing a nation, he had sacrificed his happiness to make amends. He could do it again, but he had to stop teasing himself with the fantasy of life with Lacey.

"Hafiz," Lacey said in a husky voice, "there are many reasons why I love you. You have worked hard to make up for your mistakes. You try to be a good man, a good son and a good prince. I have always admired your willpower and your strength. But your one weakness is me."

Hafiz wanted to deny it.

She slowly shook her head. "All this time I've hated the idea that I'm your one and only vice. Your weakness. But it's true. I am making you into the man you don't want to be."

"That's not true. I like who I am when I'm with you."

"You like sneaking around?" she asked. "Breaking promises? Feeling guilty because you shouldn't love a woman like me?"

"No," he admitted gruffly.

"Would you have acted this way with another woman? Would you make love to her in public?"

Hafiz wanted to lie and say yes. But even when he was known as the playboy prince, he had always been aware of his surroundings. But when he was with Lacey, nothing else mattered. It wasn't just a weakness. It was a sickness.

"You know what kind of woman I want to be?" she asked.

He knew. She never said it out loud, but he knew of her plans and dreams. Lacey wanted to be a woman surrounded by love and family.

"I can tell you that I didn't grow up thinking I wanted to be a femme fatale. I didn't want to be the kind of woman who ruined lives."

"You're not ruining my life. My—" He

stopped. He wasn't going to think it. Voice it. His royal status was part of his identity and the one true constant in his life. It was not an obstacle that kept him from being with Lacey.

"I'm a problem for you, Hafiz. What do you think is going to happen if this photo gets out? What will the sultan do?"

Hafiz gritted his teeth. He wasn't going to tell Lacey. She would try to protect him and keep him in Abu Dhabi. "I can take care of myself."

"No, that's the wrong way to go around it," Lacey said. "That's expected. You'll probably use the words that every powerful man has used when denying an affair. I will take care of this."

Hafiz's shoulders went rigid. "No, you will not."

"Why not?" Lacey's eyes lit up, and she held up her hands. Hafiz knew that look. Lacey had a plan. "This is what we're going to do. If the picture gets published, I'll take the blame."

"Not a chance."

"Listen to me, Hafiz." She placed her hand on

his arm as she pleaded. "It's so simple. I'll tell people that I saw you at this party, and I came onto you. You rejected my advances."

He wasn't going to let anyone think that his woman was an indiscriminate seductress. "The picture says otherwise."

"Pictures lie." She dismissed his words with the wave of her hand. "No one knows what happened before or after. It's very possible that I propositioned you. It's just as possible that you declined my offer."

Hafiz gave her a disbelieving look. He couldn't remember a time when he refused Lacey. "No."

She squeezed his arm. "It will work."

He placed his hand over hers. "No, it won't. I am not hiding behind a woman."

She jerked her hand away. "Excuse me?"

He leaned closer. "And no one is going to believe you."

"Yes, they will."

"Not when every gossip site is going to drag up my playboy past and follows up with my former lovers."

He felt the weight of his past on his shoulders. Why had he thought he could erase those moments? And why did it all have to be dug up now?

"Lacey, there is a very real chance that someone took a picture of us after the party." He was furious at himself that he'd put her in this position.

She blushed a bright red. "If they had a picture, they would have already used it, right?"

"No, they would hint that something even more scandalizing is coming out," Hafiz said. "Stir up interest and sell it to the highest bidder."

"Hafiz, I'm sure there aren't any more pictures," she said in a shaky voice. "We would have seen someone."

He wasn't so sure. They had been lost in their own world. "I need to call a few people and find out if someone is shopping the pictures," he said as he turned on his cell phone and walked to the door.

"Good. And I—"

He halted and turned around, stopping her with one warning look. "You will stay here."

She glared at him. "You have no say in the matter. Anyway, I have to go to work in a couple of hours."

"Promise me that you won't try to fix this," Hafiz said in a low tone. "I need you to trust me on this. Let me handle it."

"But—"

"I won't let you down."

She hesitated, and Hafiz knew what she was thinking. He had let his former mistress down. Back then, he had abandoned his woman when she was vulnerable and in need. At that time, he didn't have the power to protect what was his from the sultan. Now he did, and he wasn't going to let anything happen to Lacey.

"Fine," she said through clenched teeth. "I will hang back…for now. But if I see that you are in trouble, I am—"

"No, you won't." He didn't care what she was planning to do. He wasn't going to let it happen. Hafiz grabbed the door handle and was about

to cross the threshold when he turned around.
"And, Lacey, one of these days you will realize
that I don't need saving."

CHAPTER TWELVE

LACEY LOOKED OUT on the audience and gave a warm smile as she played the last note on the piano.

Why am I wasting my life doing this? she wondered. *Why do I still feel as if my life is on hold?*

Her smile tightened. The spotlight above her felt extraordinarily hot as sweat trickled down her spine. There were only a few people in the hotel lounge on the weekday afternoon.

That was not unusual, Lacey decided as she rose from the bench and bowed to the smattering of applause. It was common to see a few businessmen sitting in the audience at this time of day. They all had a dazed look from back-to-back meetings or constant travel.

She knew they weren't really listening to the music. If asked, they wouldn't remember her or describe her hair in a tight bun or her black lace dress. They were here because they didn't want to return to their quiet hotel rooms. They didn't want to be alone.

Lacey knew how they felt. She had struggled with loneliness before she had met Hafiz. It permeated her life and had been the theme in all the songs she had performed.

And when she met Hafiz, she had felt a connection between them. It had excited and frightened her. She didn't want to lose it. She didn't want it to end.

She glanced around the lounge and noticed Hafiz was not there. He knew when she was going to perform but he didn't stop by. Hafiz had always claimed that he enjoyed listening to her music, but now she wondered if that was just an empty compliment. Or perhaps he enjoyed it when she performed only for him.

She knew he wouldn't be there, but yet she still couldn't stop the disappointment dragging her down. Did he not show up because he was too busy or because he didn't want to be seen in the same room with her?

It shouldn't hurt. She was used to Hafiz not being part of her life. If he had shown up, she would have been unreasonably happy. Thrilled that he graced her with his presence.

And even with the decision that she wasn't going to let him treat her this way anymore, Lacey knew she would weaken her stance. She wanted him in her life no matter how little time she got with him.

Her dreams were not as grand as Hafiz's goals. Her plans for her life wouldn't lead her on the road to glory. At times what she wanted in life seemed impossible. But that didn't mean her dreams were less important than Hafiz's dreams. She needed to remember that.

What she wanted in life was to be with Hafiz. Build a life together and have a family. Create a home that was filled with love, laughter and music.

Lacey quickly got off the stage and glided between the empty tables. There was no use yearning for that kind of life. She wasn't going to get it. Not while she was on this path, waiting, hoping for Hafiz to change his mind.

Maybe she was Rapunzel. Lacey's footsteps slowed as the thought crashed through her. Oh, hell. She *was* the one who was stuck. She kept following the same pattern, waiting for a different outcome.

This was why she felt like her life was on hold. She was waiting for Prince Hafiz to reach out, take her away from her tower, and carry her away with him.

Not anymore. As much as she loved Hafiz and would greedily accept whatever he could spare, she didn't want a part-time love. She couldn't agree to sharing him.

She wanted a love that was exclusive and one that would last. She was willing to work for it, willing to give up a lot to make it happen. But she would not be his mistress or long-distance lover. She deserved more than that.

Lacey hurried through the hotel and headed for the staff housing. An enclosed garden separated the employee residences from the hotel. She usually found it peaceful walking past the fountains and ponds, inhaling the fragrance of the brightly colored flowers. Today the formal garden seemed too big.

"Lacey?"

Her pulse gave a hard kick when she heard the familiar masculine voice. She whirled around and saw Hafiz. Her heart started to pound as she stared at him. He was devastatingly handsome in his black suit. The severe lines of his jacket emphasized his broad shoulders and lean torso. He looked powerful and sophisticated. She was very aware of her cheap lace dress and secondhand shoes.

"Hafiz?" she whispered and frantically looked around the garden. "What are you doing here?"

"What do you mean?" he asked as he approached her. "I'm staying at this hotel."

"I mean you shouldn't be seen speaking to me. The last thing you need are more pictures of us together."

"The picture has been deleted," he said.

"Oh." Lacey knew that it was the wisest course of action, but getting rid of the picture bothered her. She realized it was because she had no pictures of them together. It was as if all evidence of them together had been erased.

"Why do you look upset?" Hafiz asked. "I took care of it just like I said I would."

"I had no doubt that you would be successful." Hafiz always got what he wanted. Except her. It made her wonder just how much he really wanted her in his life.

"You don't have to worry about it being released."

"I wasn't worried," she said, crossing her arms as a gentle breeze brushed against her skin. "I don't care if people know I'm with you."

Hafiz frowned. "You don't care if people know that you were a mistress?"

Did she care that people knew she didn't hold out for a wedding ring? That she accepted whatever Hafiz offered so she could be with him? No, she didn't regret those choices, but she knew she couldn't make them again.

In the past she'd thought accepting his offer to live in Rudaynah was one step toward a future together. Now she understood the rules. She either got to be his mistress, or she didn't get to be with him at all.

If he asked her to be his mistress now, she would decline. Even if he was unattached, even if he moved out of Rudaynah. It would be hard to say no, but these days she placed more value on herself and her dreams.

"I just finished working," Lacey said as she took a few steps away.

"I know," he said as he moved closer.

"I didn't see you in the lounge." Lacey bit down on her lip, preventing herself from saying anything more.

He frowned at her sharp tone as if he sensed an emotional minefield. "I wanted to be there."

"Something more important came along?" she asked with false brightness. "Something better?"

"You know why I couldn't be there."

"No, I really don't." She had automatically

accepted the belief that they couldn't be seen together, and yet, here they were alone in a garden, deep in conversation. It felt as if he chose when he could and could not see her. "Explain it to me. Why were you not there to support me?"

"Did you need my support?" he asked.

"Yes." She never asked because she didn't want to set herself up for rejection. Her parents had not taken the time to see her perform while she was in school or early in her career. Hafiz had only seen her a few times early in their relationship.

"You have performed on stage countless times," he pointed out.

"Doesn't matter. I was always there for you, behind the scenes and in the shadows. I didn't stand next to you during ceremonies and events, but I supported your work. Why don't you support mine?"

His eyes narrowed. "Where is this coming from?"

"You wouldn't understand," she said as she closed her eyes. She realized she surprised him

with her demand. It was rare to demand anything from him. She had spent so much energy
trying to be part of his life that she didn't expect
him to take part in hers.

"Lacey, the next time I'm here, I will sit in the
front row and watch your entire performance,"
he promised.

She went still. "The next time you're here?"

"I'm leaving Abu Dhabi in a few hours," he
said. "It's time for me to home."

He was going back. Lacey shouldn't be surprised, but she was struggling not to show it.
"You are returning to Rudaynah?"

"I have to go back." His tone suggested that
there had never been a question. "I'm still the
prince. I have obligations."

"And a wedding?" she bit out.

Hafiz tilted his head back and sighed. "Yes,
I am getting married."

"Why?" Lacey asked as the hopelessness
squeezed her chest. "I've seen what kind of
marriage you're entering. It's bleak and lonely.

There is no happiness, no partnership and no love. Why are you doing this?"

"Because this is what I deserve!" he said in a harsh tone.

She gulped in air as she stared at Hafiz. "You're still punishing yourself for something you did over ten years ago," she said in a daze. "Hafiz, your countrymen have forgiven you. In fact, they adore you."

"It's not about my country. Yes, I accepted an arranged marriage because it is my duty. But I don't deserve a love marriage. Not because I'm a prince. It's because of what I did to Elizabeth."

"Your mistress who had become pregnant?" she asked. "I don't understand."

"I discarded her and I denied my son. I had a chance to take care of them, but instead I abandoned them. I treated them worse than how your parents treated you."

"Don't say that," Lacey whispered. "You are nothing like my parents. You value family. Your children will be your highest priority."

"I don't deserve to become a father after what

I did. I neglected my responsibilities because I had been selfish. One day my brother will have a son, and he will become the heir to the throne."

She was stunned by his words. Lacey had always known that Hafiz would make a good father. He would be attentive but allow his children to forge their own paths and make their own mistakes.

"All this time," Lacey said, "you've been avoiding a love marriage and creating a family because of the way you treated Elizabeth?"

"Yes," he said. "It's only right."

"No, it's not. I'm sure Elizabeth has moved on."

"That doesn't matter," Hafiz replied. "My suffering doesn't end because she can accept what happened in the past. What I did was unforgivable."

"You have suffered enough," Lacey declared. "You have sacrificed your happiness for years while you've taken care of Rudaynah. You did everything you could to be the dutiful son and the perfect prince. When is it going to stop?"

"I don't know. What if the selfish and spoiled prince is the real me? What if the playboy prince is underneath the surface, ready to break free?"

"It's not," Lacey insisted. "What I see before me is the real you. Caring and loving. Strong and protective. This is the man you're supposed to be."

"I want that to be true, but I can't take that risk. I am going back to Rudaynah and marry Nabeela, who understands that this marriage is nothing more than a business arrangement."

"This is crazy!"

"But I promise, Lacey, I will be back one day."

"How? When?" She frowned. "Why?"

"Why? Because I'm not giving up on us."

Her eyes widened. "Are you saying that you want a long-distance relationship?"

"Yes," he said as he reached for her. "We did it before when you lived in St. Louis."

She snatched her hands back. "That wasn't

what it was. You kept visiting me because you couldn't stay away."

"It started out that way."

"And then you visited more frequently. Your trips were longer. But you never made the commitment."

"I was faithful to you." His eyes flashed with anger. "I haven't been interested in another woman since I met you."

"We weren't living together. Your main residence was somewhere else. And it was the same in Rudaynah. We were in the same country, the same city, but we lived separately."

"So what?"

Lacey crossed her arms and hesitated. She wasn't asking for marriage, and she wasn't asking for forever, but she knew she might be asking for too much. "If you want to be with me, then you have to make the commitment. You have to live with me."

"We can't." His answer was automatic.

"You mean, *you* can't."

"I just explained why I can't," Hafiz said. "If

you expect a commitment from me, you are setting yourself up for disappointment."

"And I don't mean living in the same town or in the same hemisphere," she continued. "We will share a home and live as a couple."

"You can't return to Rudaynah."

"I know." She rolled her shoulders back and met his gaze. "You will live elsewhere."

"You mean leave the sultanate?" He angrily barked out the word, but she could see the fear in his eyes. The fear of losing her again. "Do you understand what you are asking of me?" He splayed his hands in the air.

"Yes, I'm asking to you to make a choice." And she had a feeling that she was setting herself up for rejection. "You asked me to make the same choice when I moved to Rudaynah."

"That is different. You didn't have obligations that tied you down to one place."

"It's not different. I made a choice of staying home or being with you. I chose you."

Hafiz took a deep breath. "Lacey," he said

quietly, "I wish I could live with you. You are the only woman I've ever loved."

"But you don't want anyone to know it." She felt the first tear drip from her eyelashes, and she dashed it away with the side of her hand. "You love me as long as nothing is expected of you."

"That is not true." Hafiz's voice was gruff. "I want to take care of you. I want to be with you. Share a life together."

"You mean share *part* of your life," Lacey said. "You want to give me the occasional day or weekend. That's not good enough. I want it all."

He splayed his hands in the air. "You are asking me to do the impossible."

"Then there is nothing you can do but—" her breath hitched in her throat "—walk away."

Hafiz stared at her with incredulity. "I tried to do that, but I can't. I won't!"

"You have to," she pleaded, her tears falling unchecked. "If you really love me, if you really want the best for me, you will."

"What's best?" He flinched as if she slapped him. "Suddenly I'm not good for you?"

"You have to set me free." She didn't realize how hard it would be to say those words. Hafiz's devastated look made her want to snatch them back. It took all of her courage to continue. "Let me find a life where my needs are equal to everyone else's."

"What do you—" Hafiz's eyes lit with brutal understanding, and he recoiled from her. "You mean you want to find another man," he spat out.

"If it comes to that." Lacey knew it wasn't possible, but she couldn't let Hafiz know that, or he would continue to pursue her. "I need someone in my life who will put me first, just like I place him first. I can't have that kind of life with you."

"I have always put you first," he said in an angry hiss. "I took care of you the best way I knew how. I—" He covered his face with his hands. "I would die for you."

Lacey believed him, and it bruised her heart.

She didn't want him to die for her. She wanted to share her life with him. The thought speared her chaotic mind. Everything became clear.

She swept her tongue across her lips as her jittery heart pounded against her chest. "If it was between living with me or dying for the good of Rudaynah, which would you choose? The ultimate shame of loving me or the highest honor of serving your country?"

Hafiz was frozen in silence. She held her breath in anticipation as Hafiz dragged his hands from his face. She saw all of the emotions flickering in his ashen face. Shock. Pain. Hesitation.

"That's what I thought." She dragged the words out of her aching throat as hope shriveled up and died inside her. Hafiz might have loved her and he might have trusted her, but he couldn't be proud of her. He couldn't respect himself for loving her.

Nothing she could do would change that. She wasn't going to make the mistake of trying to earn her way. She wasn't going to think that being patient and uncomplaining would be rewarded.

"You need to leave and never come back," she said as she marched away. "Right now."

He shook his head. "I am not leaving. Not until you listen."

"I've listened, and I know nothing is going to change. I need to leave to protect myself. Goodbye, Hafiz," she said, her voice breaking as she fled.

CHAPTER THIRTEEN

SHE HAD TO protect herself. Hafiz silently leaned back in his chair and listened to the business presentation given in his conference room, but he turned Lacey's words over and over in his head. *I need to leave to protect myself.*

From him. Hafiz clenched his jaw as the hurt stung through his chest. It was that thought that had kept him up at night for the past week. Why did she think he was harmful to her? He would never touch her in anger or deny her anything. Everything he did for Lacey was to support her. Protect her.

Hadn't he proved it in Abu Dhabi when he'd kept the pictures from being released? Hadn't he spent lavishly on her throughout their affair? How did her life get worse because of him?

He was the one who needed to protect himself. He could have lost everything if their relationship had been revealed. He was addicted to Lacey Maxwell and risked everything for her. Why didn't she see that?

But instead she cut off all contact. She gave up on them. She abandoned *him*.

Hafiz wanted to believe it was for the best. She was a distraction he couldn't afford. He had almost everything he worked for just within his grasp. His work to improve the lives in the sultanate was making progress. He had made Rudaynah a wealthy country. He would regain the title of crown prince that had been stripped from him.

So why did he feel as if he had failed Lacey?

I need someone who will place me first.

Lacey's words echoed in his head. He was a prince. He could not make a person more of a priority than his country.

Because he was a prince, he was not the man she needed. The knowledge devastated him. Most women would have accepted that. Most women would have been thrilled with the arrangement he offered Lacey.

But not Lacey. She wanted the one thing he couldn't give her. No, *wouldn't* give her. His duty to the sultanate may have sounded noble, but she understood him too well. All this time he thought he was trying to make up for his past sins, but he was just as driven hiding the fact that he was a man who couldn't meet the high standards placed on him.

All he managed to prove was that he was not worthy of Lacey Maxell.

He had worked hard to make up for his mistakes, and he was a prince who was respected and admired. But was he the man he wanted to be? No. He was making the same mistakes.

Despite the punishment he had received for having a kept woman in the past, Hafiz had made Lacey his mistress. Not his girlfriend or wife. He hadn't thought she needed that status. He had treated her as a sexual convenience instead of the woman he loved.

Hafiz had known about Lacey's upbringing,

but he had done nothing to make her feel safe in the relationship. She had been neglected and abandoned. Marginalized in her family. Instead of showing how grateful he was that she was in his life, he had kept her on the sidelines of his life.

Hafiz frowned as he gave a good look at his affair with Lacey. He thought their relationship had been perfect. A dream. A fantasy. He thought he had been generous and good to Lacey, but he had failed her.

He had to fix this. Somehow he would show Lacey that she was the most important person in his life. She thought it could only be demonstrated by marriage, but that was wrong. Marriage was about alliances and property. It was about lineage and power.

He would prove to Lacey that marriage had nothing to do with love.

Lacey sighed as she tiredly unlocked the door to her apartment. The stupor that had encased her almost a week ago when she left Hafiz now felt cracked and brittle. Exhaustion had seeped in. She couldn't wait to tumble into bed, regardless of the fact that it would be cold and lonely.

She pushed the door open and stumbled to a halt as she was greeted by Damask roses everywhere. Lacey inhaled the heavy fragrance with her gasp of surprise. The front room looked like a garden with red and pink flowers.

An image splintered through her mind. St. Louis, in the hotel's penthouse suite. Hafiz dragging a rose bud along her naked body. Longing swept through her as a flush of red crept under her pale skin.

"Lacey, I have to know," her roommate Priya said as she strolled into the room, wearing wrinkled pajamas. "What have you done to deserve all these flowers?"

"They're for me?" Her stomach clenched. She'd sensed they were. Only one person would send her flowers. Only one man would make such a grand gesture. Trust Hafiz to disregard her demands and to this extent. Suddenly she was a challenge that he had to overcome. "Uh… nothing."

Priya cast a disbelieving look. "No guy goes through all this trouble without a reason," she said as she walked over to one oversized bouquet and stroked the fragile petals. "And this one is very sure he has no competition. He didn't sign the cards."

Lacey felt her mouth twist into a bittersweet smile. Hafiz didn't need to say anything because the flowers said it all. He wanted to remind her of the passion between them, the love they shared and of what she was turning her back on.

As if she was in a trance, Lacey walked from one bouquet to the next. The shades of pink and red thawed the coldness inside her. She felt the vibrant flowers questioning her choice to exist without Hafiz. Lacey sighed, knowing she should have ignored the bouquets and gone straight to bed.

"Prince Hafiz doesn't want you to forget him,"

Priya said with a sigh and placed her hands on her hips. "As if you could."

"I'm not getting back together with him."

"If you say so," her roommate said softly.

She bent her head and brushed her cheek against the soft petals. "I've learned that being with him wasn't worth the tears," she lied.

"No guy is," Priya muttered.

Lacey pressed her lips together. Hafiz was worth it. What she had really learned was that he didn't think *she* was worth the sacrifice or the struggle. Hafiz desired her, he may even believe that he loved her, but he didn't love her enough.

"I should call...and tell him to stop," Lacey said. She needed to let him know that she couldn't be wooed like the first time. She understood the rules now. Another affair with him would destroy her.

"Uh-huh." Priya rolled her eyes. "Right."

Was she kidding herself? Lacey wondered as she grabbed her cell phone from her purse and headed for her bedroom. Maybe those flowers stirred up a longing she didn't feel strong enough to deny. Maybe she was desperate to hear from Hafiz, and she was jumping on to this weak excuse. Lacey knew she should talk herself out of it, but instead she paced the floor as she called, wondering why she hadn't deleted his number. She held the phone to her ear with shaky fingers.

"Hello, Lacey."

She halted in the middle of her room. "Hafiz." She closed her eyes, tears instantly welling. Her heartbeats stuttered as a shiver swept through her. He sounded so close to her, as if his mouth was pressed against her ear, ready to whisper sweet nothings. Lacey curled her head into her shoulders, wanting to hold on to the feeling, wanting it to be real. "Thank you for the flowers, but I don't think you should be sending me presents," she said huskily. She gritted her teeth. She needed to be firm.

"Why?" His voice was silky and smooth, heating her body from the inside out.

Lacey frowned. Why? Was he kidding? Wasn't

it obvious? "Because it's not—" she resumed pacing as she searched for the word "—appropriate."

"When have we ever been appropriate?" Hafiz's sexy chuckle weakened her knees.

She had to follow through and tell him to stop. She had to be strong. "I mean it," she said sternly, hoping he didn't catch the slight waver. "I don't want anything from you."

"That's not true."

She closed her eyes as his low voice made her skin tingle. It wasn't true. She wanted everything from him. But why would he give it to her? After a year of eagerly accepting whatever he offered, she knew Hafiz thought he could wear her down. That this was some sort of negotiation.

She couldn't live that way anymore. She deserved more. She deserved everything. She refused to settle.

"I've already told you that I'm not interested in married men."

Hafiz was quiet for a moment. "What if I broke the engagement?" he asked.

Her breath hitched in her throat. "Would you?" Her knees started to wobble. Was it because of her? Was he going to give the palace an ultimatum? "Could you?"

"I'm not interested in marriage."

"Oh." She sank on the bed. So many emotions fought inside her, struggling to surface, that they felt as if they would burst through her skin. Hope soared through her, and realization pulled her down. He may no longer be the playboy prince, but he also had no interest in marriage. With her, with anyone.

As much as she didn't want him to get married, she also wanted to weep because she couldn't be with him and never would. "But it's only a matter of time before the palace can prove why marriage is necessary."

"I don't need a wife to be a good prince."

"Now, there you are wrong," Lacey said as she lay down on the bed and drew her knees to her stomach. "You need a woman at your side. A family of your own."

"I had that with you," he reminded her, his voice filled with such tenderness that she ached. "But Rudaynah wouldn't recognize it like that. The palace would never accept it."

And the ties that bound him to Rudaynah were too powerful for her to cut. Hafiz might withstand the burdens placed on him, but not if he held on to her. Lacey winced with pain as she had to make a decision, her face already wet with tears. She had to be the strong one, or they both were headed for destruction.

She took a deep breath. She could do this. She had to do this and take the brunt of the fall. Even if it meant she would wither and die, she would do it, as long as Hafiz thrived and flourished. "What we had was good." She choked out the words. "But we can never recapture it."

"Lacey?" Hafiz asked in an urgent tone.

"No more presents." She thought she was going to gag on her tears. "No more trying to… No more.…" She disconnected the call and turned off the phone.

Lacey curled up into a ball as her spirit howled with agony. She clutched the phone, the last tangible connection she had with Hafiz, to her chest. Her weary body convulsed as she cried.

She wished she could disintegrate. But she knew the ramifications of her decision were just beginning. She had to live without Hafiz, and she had to be ruthless about it. Starting now. It meant leaving Abu Dhabi. Tonight. Without a trace. Without hope.

Hafiz stood at the arched window and watched the laborers set up the decorations along the route to the palace. The colorful flags and banners celebrated his upcoming nuptials while street vendors displayed wedding souvenirs.

He wished he could be as excited about the week-long ceremony. Maybe, if it had been a different bride. A woman with copper hair and a smile that warmed his heart. A woman he loved and who fiercely loved him in return.

"Having second thoughts?"

He turned to the sound of his brother's voice. From the concern lining the crown prince's face, Hafiz knew he must look like hell.

Ashraf strode down the open hallway, the desert morning wind tugging his white robe. His younger brother looked how a crown prince should. Hafiz felt scruffy and tarnished in comparison in his tunic and jeans.

That was no surprise. Ashraf was the perfect son. The perfect prince. And did it all effortlessly when Hafiz failed spectacularly.

While Ashraf embraced tradition, Hafiz always questioned it. Hafiz was tempted by the world outside of Rudaynah, and Ashraf preferred to stay home. Hafiz couldn't resist the charms of an inappropriate woman. From all accounts, his brother lived like a monk, nothing distracting him as he fulfilled the role of the heir apparent. One day he would be the benevolent sultan this country needed. Rudaynah would be in good hands with Ashraf on the throne.

"I was thinking about something else," Hafiz said.

"*Someone* else. A woman," Ashraf guessed. "And from the look in your eyes, not the woman you are about to marry."

Hafiz nodded. "Her name is Lacey Maxwell."

No recognition flickered in his brother's eyes. "Who is she?"

"She's my..." Mistress? The term bothered Hafiz. It had been Lacey's status, but the word minimized her place in his life. She was not a sexual plaything. The label of mistress didn't describe her generous spirit or inquisitive mind. It didn't explain how important she had been in his life.

"She's yours," Ashraf said simply.

"She should be my bride." It hurt to say it. He hadn't said it to Lacey, and now it was too late. He gave voice to the idea, even though he knew it couldn't happen. And yet...Hafiz pushed away from the window.

"I know that look," Ashraf said. "Whatever you're thinking, just forget about it."

"You don't know what's going through my mind," Hafiz said with a scowl.

Ashraf grabbed Hafiz's arm. "Back out of this wedding and you could lose everything."

Okay, so his brother was a mind reader. "I've already lost everything," Hafiz replied.

"Not quite. This is just wedding nerves," Ashraf said, his fingers biting into Hafiz's arm. "Marry the sultan's choice and keep this Lacey Maxwell on the side."

"No, she deserves better. She should be the one who should have my family name. I don't want to hide how I feel about her anymore."

"Listen to me, Hafiz. I'm giving you advice even though it's against my best interest," Ashraf said. "I understand you will be made crown prince once you marry."

The pause between them sat uncomfortably on Hafiz. "Does everyone know about that agreement?" he finally asked. "Don't worry,

Ashraf. Knowing the sultan, he will find a loophole to prevent that from happening."

"Typical Hafiz," Ashraf muttered. "You always think someone is going to betray you. That they are destined to fail you."

"I'm cautious," Hafiz corrected. "The more I know of this world and the more I understand people, I become more cautious."

"That shouldn't include your family." The shadows darkened on his face. "Despite what you may think, I didn't betray you when I became crown prince. I had to preserve the line of succession."

Hafiz drew back, astounded by the guilt stamped on his brother's face. "I don't blame you. I blame myself. I'm sorry you were dragged into this. In fact—" Hafiz tilted his head as a thought occurred to him "—you were affected most of all by what happened."

"You have the chance to redeem yourself and reclaim the title of crown prince."

"Maybe I don't want it anymore," Hafiz said. "Maybe I found something better."

"Like the title of Lacey's husband?" Ashraf asked in disbelief.

He wasn't worthy of that title. He had disappointed Lacey too many times. But he was willing to spend the rest of his life earning the right to be with her.

"You are very close to regaining your birthright," his brother said. "Don't ruin it now."

He was very aware of completing his ten-year quest, and yet he didn't think it was going to happen. He didn't believe it should happen. "Sometimes I think ruling Rudaynah was never my destiny."

"What has gotten into you?" Ashraf asked. "This isn't you talking. This is Lacey."

Lacey made him look at his life differently. She showed him what really mattered. "Perhaps I was only supposed to hold on to the crown prince title temporarily."

Ashraf gave him a suspicious look. "Do you really believe this, or are you trying to talk yourself into giving it up again?"

"I was holding on to the title until you were ready."

"You were born a crown prince," Ashraf said, his voice rising with anger. "You were destined to take care of this country, just like you were destined to marry for duty."

"I marry tomorrow," Hafiz said, grimacing.

His brother studied him carefully. "If you don't marry, you will be exiled. For life."

Hafiz flinched. He lifted his head and allowed the cool breeze to glide across his skin. Inhaling the scent of palm trees and sand warmed from the sun, he felt the land beckon his Bedouin blood. He opened his eyes and stared at the dunes in the distance, feeling the depth of his connection to his ancestors.

"Marry their choice of bride." Ashraf gave him a firm shake. "You were going to before. What could possibly have changed?"

"I found out what life was like without Lacey." Life without any contact with his woman was slowly destroying him. Hafiz returned his attention to the horizon, wondering where she could be. She'd vanished, sending her message loud and clear. *Don't follow me. Don't find me. Get on with your life.*

"Do you have any idea what life will be like without Rudaynah?" Ashraf asked.

Living away from the land he loved was a misery all of its own. No matter where he had been and how much he enjoyed his travels, his heart always heard the call from the land of his people. Sometimes the ancient call brushed against him like a haunting song. Other times, it crashed against him with the beat of tribal drums. "I've lived elsewhere," Hafiz finally said.

"But always knowing that you could return in an instant," Ashraf pointed out.

Hafiz closed his eyes, and his shoulders sagged. Was he wrong to consider life with Lacey when she'd made it clear she'd moved on without him? Was it foolish to hope for the impossible or was his faith in his love being tested?

"No matter what happens, you are my brother, and that will never change."

Hafiz inhaled sharply as the emotion welled in his chest. Ashraf would never know how important it was to hear those words. He stepped forward and embraced his brother.

Ashraf returned the embrace. "And when I reign," he promised fiercely, "you will be invited back to Rudaynah with open arms."

"Thank you." His words were muffled into his brother's shoulders.

Ashraf stepped away and met his brother's gaze. "But our father could reign for years. Decades. Are you willing to risk exile for that long?"

Hafiz realized he couldn't answer that. What did that say about him and the strength of his love for Lacey? "I don't know."

"Rudaynah is a part of you," his brother reminded him. "You can't deny that."

"But Lacey is a part of me, as well." To deny that was to refuse the man he was. The man he could potentially be.

"Then for the next twenty-four hours you need to decide which one you can live without." Ashraf pressed his lips together as his stark face tightened with apprehension. "Because this time, my brother, there's no second chance."

CHAPTER FOURTEEN

THE ELEGANT SURROUNDINGS in the lounge seemed a world away from the trendy night-clubs and blues bars of her past. She *was* a world away, Lacey decided as her fingers flew over the piano keys. Istanbul was a culturally diverse city, but it wasn't home.

Home. Lacey gave a slight shake of her head. A simple word but a complicated idea. Home wasn't St. Louis. She had no family or connection there. Nor was it Abu Dhabi. While she had friends in the beautiful city, she didn't feel as if she had belonged.

She chose to move to Istanbul because it felt like a bridge between Hafiz's world and hers. She tried to take the changes in stride, but she felt the loss of everything familiar. Of everything she'd left behind.

The only time she had felt at peace was in the penthouse apartment in Rudaynah. Lacey didn't know why she missed that place so much. She had been hidden and isolated. She couldn't count on the basic necessities. She'd had difficulty living in the sultanate, but that apartment had been the one place where she and Hafiz could be together.

She wondered what had happened to the apartment. Hafiz undoubtedly got rid of it. He no longer needed a hideaway, since he would live in the palace with his wife.

Lacey's fingers paused on the piano keys for a moment as the pain ripped through her. She continued to play, her touch a little harder, as she imagined Hafiz as a newlywed.

The last news she read about Rudaynah was about the preparations for his wedding. After that, she stopped searching for information about the sultanate. It didn't matter if his marriage was arranged or if his bride was incompatible. Hafiz would do whatever it took to make the marriage work. Even give up the woman he loved.

When the audience applauded while the last mournful note clung to the air, a uniformed waiter approached the piano. "A request." He presented his silver serving tray with a flourish.

The Damask rose lying on the cream card caught her attention. The sight of the pale pink flower was like a punch in the stomach. They were just like the roses Hafiz used to send her.

Lacey swallowed and hesitated before she took it from the waiter. Her hands trembled as she nestled the fragrant flower between her fingers before picking up the card.

She stared at bold slashes in black ink. Lacey blinked, scrunching her eyes closed before opening them wide. She stared incomprehensively at Hafiz's handwriting.

It couldn't be. It looked like Hafiz's scrawl only because she was thinking of him. She was always thinking of him. But the request was for the song Hafiz always wanted her play. It had been their song.

The clink of stemware clashed in her ears. The murmur of different languages boomed in her head. She wet her suddenly dry lips with the tip of her tongue. "Where did you get this?" she asked huskily. She felt as if she was paralyzed with shock.

"That man." Lacey's heart leaped into her throat as the blood roared in her ears. From the corner of her eyes, she saw the waiter pointed in the direction of a window that offered a breathtaking view of the Bosphorus strait. "Well, the man who had been over there," he said with a shrug and left.

Lacey's shoulders tightened, and her pulse continued to pound a staccato beat. Had it been Hafiz? If so, then why did he leave once he found her? Had he given into temptation to see her one more time and thought better of it? She couldn't stop the pang of betrayal even when she wanted him to stay away.

Lacey cast a furtive glance around the lounge, ignoring the disappointment that flooded her bones. She didn't understand how Hafiz had found her. She thought she had made it impossible for him to follow, but then the prince never gave up on a challenge. The more difficult the test, the more determined he was to conquer.

She returned her attention to the rose in her hands. She thought she would never hear from Hafiz again. She had been his vice and the one thing in the way of his goals. No matter what she did, she could never give him what he needed.

This time he had stayed away longer. She knew it was because of his upcoming wedding. It had been ridiculously easy to avoid all news sources after that tidbit of information. She wouldn't have been able to look at his wedding pictures or cope with comparing herself and his chosen bride. But why did he seek her out? Was the pull just too strong to deny?

Rubbing the rose petals with short, agitated strokes, Lacey gave into temptation and brought the exquisite flower to her nose. Inhaling the delicate fragrance, she relived everything from the instant Hafiz invaded her life to the moment she'd retreated from his.

Regret seized her heart until the last of her strength oozed out. With clumsy fingers, Lacey set the pink flower aside on the grand piano. She couldn't cope with the sweet ache of remembering.

Her gaze fell upon the card again, wincing at the song title. The lyrics had captured how she felt about Hafiz. About them. She'd had so much faith in their love. She had believed anything was possible.

Now she knew better. Lacey wanted to crumple the card in her fists and toss it away. She knew the song by heart, had sung it to Hafiz countless times, but she no longer had the resilience to play the song. It held a glimpse of her innocent, carefree days. It was a testament of her naïve love.

And she still loved Hafiz. That was how naïve she truly was. Even though he was forbidden, married and out of reach, she still loved him.

Her love was actually stronger than when she

first played the song. It might be as battered and bruised as her heart, but her feelings reached a depth she couldn't have even imagined a year ago.

Lacey paused at the thought, her fingers curved over the ivory keys. She couldn't play it. Not now, not here. This was a song just for him, not for a roomful of strangers. She would only bare her soul for Hafiz.

She *wouldn't* play it, Lacey decided, despite his request. Even if he were here, she wouldn't cave. If he were watching over her, she would play him a different song, one that offered another message but still held a poignant memory. The song she played when they first met.

Her determination wavered as the first few chords twanged deep in her heart. She would have stopped altogether, but an inner need overrode her misery, guiding her through the song. Her smoky voice was coaxed out of her raw throat, occasionally hitching and breaking with emotion. She closed her eyes, fighting back the tears as the last note was wrung out of her, depleting her remaining strength.

The enthusiastic applause sounded far away when she felt a shadow fall over her. Lacey froze, instinctively ducking her chin. She knew who was standing next to her before she inhaled a trace of the familiar scent of sandalwood.

Lacey was reluctant to look up. She wasn't strong enough to see Hafiz and let go of him again. But she also wasn't strong enough to deny herself one more glance.

Cautiously opening her eyes, Lacey saw the expensive leather shoe on the traditional Persian rug. Her chest tightened as her gaze traveled along the black pinstripe trousers. She remembered every inch of Hafiz. The crimson red tie lay flat against his muscular chest, and the suit jacket stretched against his powerful shoulders.

Her pulse skipped hard as she looked at Hafiz's face. Her skin flushed as she stared at his harsh, lean features. When she looked into his eyes, Lacey felt the full force of his magnetic power crash over her.

Hope and devastation escaped her fractured heart. *Hafiz.*

She couldn't turn away. "What are you doing here?" Her voice croaked.

"Why didn't you play my request?" he asked softly. His voice skittered across her skin, blanketing it with goose bumps.

Lacey gnawed her bottom lip. She didn't expect the gentleness. His reticence was surprising. In fact, it bothered her. Where was the primal man who made a fierce claim on her?

She cringed as she remembered how she'd misunderstood his motives the last time he sought her out. She wasn't going to repeat that mistake. "That's not an answer," she said as she reached for the flower.

Hafiz's watchful eyes made her feel awkward. Her simple black dress suddenly felt tight against her chest and hips. The silky fabric grazed against her sensitive skin.

"When are you taking your break?" he asked.

"Now." She covered the keys and stood up abruptly. How could she work when he was nearby? At the moment, she didn't care if she received a reprimand for her boss or got docked in pay. "What are you doing here?" she repeated as she stepped away from the piano.

He arched his eyebrow in warning. "I'm here for you."

Lacey's brisk stride faltered when she heard the words she craved. But she knew better. There had to be a catch, a dark side to her deepest wish. She kept walking and sensed him following her.

"Hafiz, we've been through this," she said, grateful for her firm tone that came out of nowhere. "I am not available every time you're in town. I'm not a one-night stand. And I don't sleep with married men."

"I'm not married."

Lacey whirled around and stared at Hafiz. "What? How is the possible?"

"Is that why you didn't play my request?" his voice rumbled.

The rose threatened to snap, and she relaxed

her grip. "No. Why are you not married? You were supposed to have your wedding after Eid."

"I refused." A shadow flickered in his dark eyes. Lacey had a feeling his refusal wasn't as easy as he made it sound.

"When? Why? I don't understand. You had to. There was no way out of it."

"I found a way." Hafiz dipped his head next to hers. "Why didn't you play my request?" He was so close, sending a burst of sensations spraying through her veins. "Because you thought I was married?"

Lacey stopped in front of the lounge's entrance and folded her arms across her chest. He wasn't married. The relief swirled inside her, only to be pulled down by a heavy sadness. One day Hafiz would have to marry, and she wouldn't be the bride.

"Did you forget the words to the song?" he asked softly. "Like you tried to forget us?"

She didn't know if it would be wise to explain anything. To encourage a love that was impossible. "You wouldn't understand," she finally said.

"You don't know that," he said as he placed his large hand against the gentle swell of her hip. The contact nearly undid her. Lacey stiffened, fighting the urge to sway into his body and melt against his heat.

She needed to calm down before her heart splintered. Lacey cleared her throat. "I don't play that song anymore. It reminds me of our time together."

His fingers flexed against her spine. "And you regret what we had?" Hafiz's penetrating eyes made her feel vulnerable and exposed. "Do you regret loving me?"

Lacey exhaled wearily. Nothing could be further from the truth. In a way, her life would be so much easier if she regretted her love. "I told you that you wouldn't understand," she said as she strode away.

She didn't get very far. Before she knew it, her back was pressed against one of the alabaster columns. The Damask rose fluttered to

the champagne-colored carpet as Hafiz barri-
caded her with his strong arms. Her eyes widened anxiously as he leaned into her. "Make me
understand," he growled.

The anguish deepened the lines of his stark
face, and she struggled with the wrenching need
to erase it from him altogether. Lacey tilted
her head in the direction of the piano. "I don't
play that song because it's about you. How you
changed my life, how you changed me. How
much you mean to me and what I would do
to keep you." She pressed her clammy palms
against the column, but they streaked against
the cool, slick surface. "And that is why it belongs *only* to you."

Comprehension flashed through his bronze
eyes. "Ah." Hafiz straightened and removed his
hands from the alabaster.

Lacey frowned at his sudden retreat. She'd
revealed more than she was comfortable with,
and this was how he responded. "Ah, what?"
she asked defensively, doing her best not to feel

slighted. Why was he pulling away? "I knew you wouldn't understand."

"No, I do." The corner of mouth slowly slanted up. "It's how I feel when I give you this."

She watched with growing alarm as he removed his royal ring from his finger. The gold caught the light. Lacey stared at it, transfixed, unable to move until Hafiz grasped her wrist.

Lacey bunched her hand up into a fist. "What are you doing?" she asked in a scandalized whisper. She struggled to keep her arm flat against the column.

"I'm giving you my ring." He easily plucked her hand and moved it closer to him.

Her knuckles whitened as her tension grew. There was no way she was going to let him. She knew the rules, but she could only imagine the consequences of breaking them. "But, but—it's a royal ring." She gestured wildly at it. "Only someone born into royalty is allowed to wear it."

"And," Hafiz added as he leisurely caressed

her fingers, enticing them to unfurl, "I'm allowed to give it to the woman I want to marry."

Lacey's hand tightened, her short fingernails digging into her palm. Her mouth gaped open as the remainder of her argument dissolved on her tongue. "Marry?"

"Yes." His gaze ensnared her. The depths challenged. Tempted. Pleaded. "Marry me, Lacey."

"I—I—" she spluttered, unable to connect two words together. Her heartbeat drummed painfully against her breastbone. "I…can't."

"Why not?" Hafiz didn't sound crestfallen. His taunting tone indicated that he was primed and ready to argue. And win.

Her gaze clung on to the ring. It looked big and heavy. It belonged on Hafiz's hand, not hers.

"I'm not from the right family," she blurted out. She knew her shortcomings.

"I disagree," Hafiz said confidently. "You are the only family I need. Together we will create the home we always wanted."

And he would give it to her. He would be loving and protective. Hafiz would do everything in his power to make her feel safe and secure.

She felt herself weakening, but she couldn't let that happen. She had to be strong. Strong enough for the both of them. Lacey struggled to voice another reason. "I'm your mistress."

"You are my heart," he corrected in a husky voice. "Marry me."

"I can't marry you." Her firm statement trailed off in a whimper. She frowned ferociously and tried again. "I can't return to Rudaynah."

His hand stilled against hers. "Neither can I," he confessed.

His words froze her racing thoughts. Hafiz couldn't return to Rudaynah? What was he saying? "What?" The startled question tore past her lips as she stared at him with horror.

"I've been exiled." He broke eye contact, the frown lines burrowing into his forehead. "Banished for life."

Her hand fell from his. "Why?" she cried out, but instinctively she knew. "Because of me?" She sagged against the column as tears burned her throat and eyes. Her body threatened to collapse into a broken heap on to the floor.

"Because I refuse to give you up again," Hafiz said, his voice rough with emotion. "I was given the choice to remain in my homeland or be with you. I chose you."

Hafiz chose her. He gave up everything he wanted for her. It didn't make her feel triumphant. The news destroyed her. Lacey struggled to contain the sob rising in her throat. "You shouldn't have done that."

"I don't want to stay in Rudaynah if I can't have you at my side."

She wanted to be at his side, but not if it cost him his world. "You say that now, but one day you're…"

"I refuse to hide how I feel about you, Lacey," Hafiz said in a low voice as his eyes flashed with determination. "I have nothing to be ashamed about."

"How can you say that? After all you did, you didn't get the respect you deserve. Your father exiled you." Lacey cringed as she said those words. She knew how important his status was to Hafiz.

She'd sacrificed everything, but she wasn't able to give Hafiz the one thing he needed. He hadn't redeemed himself in the eyes of his family. He would never gain the recognition that belonged to him.

Lacey covered her face with her hands. She didn't want this to happen. She had done everything in her power to prevent Hafiz from losing the world he fought so hard to keep.

"Hafiz, you can't give up being a prince," she begged. "Not for me. Not for anyone. It's who you are."

"No, it's not." His voice was clear and steady. "I am myself, I am who I want to be, when I am with you."

"No… No…"

"I'm not fully alive unless I'm with you," he said as he wrapped his fingers around her wrists and lowered her hands. "I'm not myself when you are not around. I love you, Lacey."

Tears dampened her eyelashes. "That can't be," she whispered. "It's impossible."

He cupped his hand against her cheek. The gentle touch contrasted with the demand in his eyes. "All I know is that this ring belongs only to you. *I* belong only to you." He held the glittering royal ring in front of her.

She slowly shook her head. "Hafiz…" Her eyes widened when he bent down on one knee in front of her.

"Lacey Maxwell, will you do me the honor of marrying me?"

EPILOGUE

"LACEY, WHERE ARE you?" Hafiz looked over the assembly of dignitaries that crowded the throne room and spotted his wife lurking in the shadows. As she turned, the diamonds in her hair shimmered under the chandelier lights.

Pride swelled in his chest as she made her way through the sea of evening gowns and military uniforms. Hafiz watched statesmen and socialites respectfully lower their heads when she passed, but his attention was focused on his woman.

It amazed him how Lacey's regal image concealed her passionate nature. Just thinking about it, he was tempted to sink his fingers in her copper red hair and pull down the sophisticated chignon. The rose taffeta caftan encrusted with iridescent pearls teased his senses as it skimmed her curves with each step she took.

When Lacey drew close, he captured her hand. "The coronation is about to start," Hafiz informed her and entwined his fingers with hers.

Lacey's uncertain smile tugged at his heart. He swore it gleamed more brightly than any jewel or medal in the room. "I'm sure the vizier said I'm not supposed to be here."

"You are right where you belong." He made a mental note to give the adviser a more explicit explanation of the new protocol. No one was going to hide his woman. No one was going to separate him from his wife.

The first few notes of the procession march filtered through the throne room. Exhilaration pressed against his chest. Soon Ashraf would be crowned sultan, and then he and his brother would bring Rudaynah to its full glory. The revitalizing plans that Hafiz dreamt for years could now be realized.

Lacey cast a troubled glance at the empty throne. "Do you regret—"

He shook his head. "No, I have everything I want," he replied truthfully. Most importantly, he had Lacey. He shared a life with the woman he loved and trusted.

She also helped him realize that he didn't need a royal title to take care of his country-men. In fact, he was more successful without the restraint of royal protocols and rituals. For the past few years they'd traveled worldwide while promoting the Sultanate of Rudaynah's resources to other countries and international businesses.

And now with the passing of his father, Hafiz could return to Rudaynah any time he wanted.

It had been a bittersweet homecoming. Hafiz had felt like a stranger in his own country until Lacey lured him to the dunes. She knew that once he visited the desert, he would reconnect with the land.

The corner of his mouth kicked up in a wicked smile as he remembered how he and Lacey had spent those cold desert nights. His mind buzzed with anticipation as he rested his hand on her stomach. It was fate to have his first child conceived in Rudaynah.

Lacey's eyes widened from his possessive touch. "Stop that!" she whispered fiercely as she tried to dislodge his hand with a subtle push. "The formal announcement isn't until the end of the month. People will speculate."

Hafiz lowered his head and brushed his mouth against hers. "Let them talk."

* * * * *

MILLS & BOON®
Large Print – February 2015

AN HEIRESS FOR HIS EMPIRE
Lucy Monroe

HIS FOR A PRICE
Caitlin Crews

COMMANDED BY THE SHEIKH
Kate Hewitt

THE VALQUEZ BRIDE
Melanie Milburne

THE UNCOMPROMISING ITALIAN
Cathy Williams

PRINCE HAFIZ'S ONLY VICE
Susanna Carr

A DEAL BEFORE THE ALTAR
Rachael Thomas

THE BILLIONAIRE IN DISGUISE
Soraya Lane

THE UNEXPECTED HONEYMOON
Barbara Wallace

A PRINCESS BY CHRISTMAS
Jennifer Faye

HIS RELUCTANT CINDERELLA
Jessica Gilmore

MILLS & BOON®
Large Print – March 2015

A VIRGIN FOR HIS PRIZE
Lucy Monroe

THE VALQUEZ SEDUCTION
Melanie Milburne

PROTECTING THE DESERT PRINCESS
Carol Marinelli

ONE NIGHT WITH MORELLI
Kim Lawrence

TO DEFY A SHEIKH
Maisey Yates

THE RUSSIAN'S ACQUISITION
Dani Collins

THE TRUE KING OF DAHAAR
Tara Pammi

THE TWELVE DATES OF CHRISTMAS
Susan Meier

AT THE CHATEAU FOR CHRISTMAS
Rebecca Winters

A VERY SPECIAL HOLIDAY GIFT
Barbara Hannay

A NEW YEAR MARRIAGE PROPOSAL
Kate Hardy

0215 Rom LP